TONOPAH RANGE

Center Point
Large Print

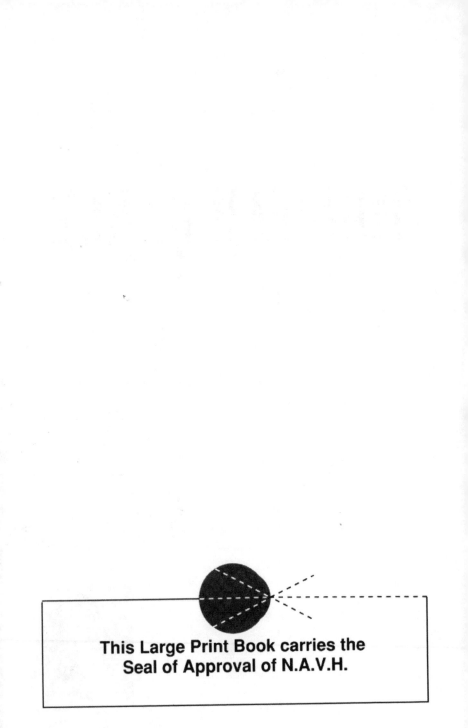

**This Large Print Book carries the
Seal of Approval of N.A.V.H.**

TONOPAH RANGE

Western Stories

Alan LeMay

CENTER POINT LARGE PRINT
THORNDIKE, MAINE

This Center Point Large Print edition
is published in the year 2015 in conjunction with
Golden West Literary Agency.

The text of this Large Print edition is unabridged.
In other aspects, this book may vary
from the original edition.
Printed in the United States of America
on permanent paper.
Set in 16-point Times New Roman type.

ISBN: 978-1-62899-397-4 (hardcover)
ISBN: 978-1-62899-401-8 (paperback)

Library of Congress Cataloging-in-Publication Data

Le May, Alan, 1899–1964.
[Short stories. Selections]
Tonopah Range : western stories / Alan LeMay.
pages ; cm
Summary: "After finding a dead man in the street, drifters Missouri
Sloper and Elmer Law decide to help discover the identity of the murder
in the title Western story. Five other short stories with unexpected
endings are also included"—Provided by publisher.
ISBN 978-1-62899-397-4 (hardcover : alk. paper)
ISBN 978-1-62899-401-8 (pbk. : alk. paper)
I. Le May, Alan, 1899–1964. Tonopah Range. II. Title.
PS3523.E513A6 2015
813′.54—dc23
2014037701

Table of Contents

Foreword

Alan (Brown) LeMay, author of such classic Western novels as *The Searchers* (Harper, 1954) and *The Unforgiven* (Harper, 1957), numerous other Western novels and stories, screenwriter, and occasionally a film producer and director was born in Indianapolis, Indiana, on June 3, 1899. He attended Stetson University in DeLand, Florida, in 1916. In 1918 he joined the U.S. Army Infantry and was commissioned in the American Expeditionary Force with the rank of 2nd lieutenant. Following his military service, he completed his education at the University of Chicago where he was graduated with a Bachelor's degree in 1922. He served as a 1st lieutenant with the Illinois National Guard in the years 1923–1924. While still in college, his short story, "Circles in the Sky," was accepted and appeared in Street & Smith's *Detective Story Magazine* (12/30/19). "Hullabaloo" appeared the same month as his graduation in *Adventure* (6/30/22). Later that year "The Brass Dolphin" appeared in *Adventure* (7/10/22) and "Ghost Lanterns" in *Adventure* (12/20/22). He married Esther Skinner on August 9, 1922. Two children were born as a result of this union, a daughter, Joan Skinner LeMay called Jody, on January 10, 1926, and a son, Dan Brown LeMay, on June 1,

1929. This marriage ended in divorce in 1938. He married Arlene Hoffman on July 22, 1939 and two children were adopted by the couple, a daughter, Molly LeMay, on September 13, 1945 and a son, Mark Logan LeMay, on April 29, 1947.

LeMay was a prolific contributor to the magazine markets in the mid 1920s. Although he did occasionally sell Western fiction to Street & Smith's *Western Story Magazine*, *Adventure* remained one of his most important markets during this decade. However, "Needin' Help Bad" in *Western Story Magazine* (9/20/24) is a short, short story that anticipates the many that LeMay would write in this length for *Collier's* in the 1930s. Newt Walker comes to an old man's shack in the Idaho mountains. He's famished, limping, without a horse. After eating the old man's grub, he asks the old man to hide him from the sheriff and his posse. The old man knows that a man named Newt Walker shot George Slade in the back, but Walker insists it was in self-defense. The old man refuses to hide the fugitive. George Slade was his son. The story ends with the sound of the sheriff's posse arriving while Walker and the old man stare fixedly at the six-gun on the table before them.

In 1927 and 1928 LeMay published a series of related humorous stories about two characters, Henry Clay Montgomery and Arthur B. Grimes, the latter known as Bug Eye, in *Adventure* and *Short Stories* that would later be expanded to form his novel, *Bug Eye* (Farrar and Rinehart, 1931). The year 1927 found him, in fact, at the height of his powers. In addition to the Bug Eye stories, his first Western novel to be published in book form, *Painted Ponies* (Doran, 1927), was serialized in *Adventure* in four parts in January and February of that year and his novel set along the Mississippi, *Old Father of Waters* (Doubleday, Doran, 1928), was serialized in the magazine in five parts, beginning in September. *Pelican Coast* (Doubleday, Doran, 1929) is set in New Orleans during the time of pirate Jean Lafitte, an exotic and colorful period rarely touched upon in historical fiction.

Painted Ponies is an important Western novel for LeMay, not only for its own merits but, in retrospect, also because it anticipated the themes and preoccupations of LeMay's finest work which came in the decade of the 1950s, just as *Old Father of Waters* set in 1858 and concerned with Mississippi riverboats anticipates the iconography and setting of his final novel, *By Dim and Flaring Lamps* (Harper, 1962). *Painted Ponies* in general follows the narrative structure employed decades later in the Will Henry novels; in this instance the trek of the Cheyenne Indians from their reservation in the Southwest back to their homeland in the Black Hills is interwoven with events in the lives of the fictional characters. Such LeMay themes as the stigma of having Indian blood from

The Unforgiven and the indomitable fanaticism of a quest from *The Searchers* are apparent already in embryonic form.

In *Painted Ponies*, Slide Morgan rides into Roaring River and wins $4,000 at roulette. Morgan is told to get out of town since Abner Cade, who owns the saloon, and his brother Lew Cade, are the leaders of the Vigilantes and they have propitiously identified Morgan as answering the description of an escaped half-breed. Morgan goes to work briefly for John Chase and falls in love with Chase's daughter, Nancy. He hides his winnings under the floorboards of the bunkhouse. Lew Cade, playing on Chase's hatred of anything the least tainted with Indian, informs him that Morgan is a half-breed on the run. Chase discharges Morgan on the strength of this allegation. When Morgan sees Lew embracing Nancy, he has a fight with him in which he hits Cade with his six-gun. The blow kills Lew Cade. From this point on Morgan becomes a fugitive with Abner Cade persistently and relentlessly on his back trail.

In his effort to elude Cade, Morgan falls in with the Cheyennes who are in the midst of their northward trek. Several of the band are well characterized. Partridge Geer, the man who raised Morgan as a boy, was the one who taught him the Cheyenne language and so Slide is able to communicate with the Indians in their language. Geer's rôle in the story is that of the old wise man.

" 'The more a man learns,' " he reflects, " 'the less he finds out.' " It is Geer who tells Slide Morgan: " 'I got on to how to get the confidence of the Injuns in the first place. Simple, too. So simple nearly ever'body missed it but me. Treat 'em square. That's th' secret they've all missed but me.' " The parallel plotting, as it progresses, develops two pursuit stories.

"The men of the prairie . . . lived their lives absorbed in the perpetual difficulties at hand," LeMay opined near the end of this story. "Yet the moods of the prairie carved their faces with deep leathery lines, twisted their backs, and did for them in the end. The faces of the Indians were moulded by the prairie, sharp, hard faces, at once whetted and blunted by privation. The whites who scraped a living out of the prairie came to look like Indians, and the Indians looked like hunted hunters, men who had always fought for their lives. . . ." LeMay's sympathies are clearly with the Cheyennes, rather than with the pursuing U.S. Cavalry, and the most moving chapter in the novel is that concerned with the Cheyennes' defeat in battle. "Reluctantly perhaps, but truly nevertheless, the United States uniform was riding forth to confirm the destruction of women and children, just as surely as they were raising their rifles against Dull Knife's braves." However, this is not to say that LeMay made no effort to show both sides of the conflict, since he surely did, and in this he was decades before the time when such balanced perspectives came into vogue in the Western story.

By 1929 LeMay had broken into the higher-paying slick magazines with "Loan of a Gun" in *Collier's* (2/23/29), collected in *The Bells of San Juan* (Five Star Westerns, 2001). His fiction in the 1930s was, in fact, almost as much a staple in *Collier's* as was that of Ernest Haycox. Feeling that he should reserve his Alan LeMay byline for *Collier's* and his novels, as early as 1930 he published fact articles in *Adventure* under the pseudonym Whiskers Beck, actually among his last contributions to this magazine which concluded finally with "The Killer in the Chute" in *Adventure* (7/1/32), collected in *West of Nowhere* (Five Star Westerns, 2002). His Western fiction published in pulp magazines, beginning with "Lawman's Debt" in *Dime Western* (5/34), appeared under the anagrammatic byline Alan M. Emley. He was still using this byline as late as 1944 in fiction he wrote for *Thrilling Ranch Stories*, *Texas Rangers*, and *Thrilling Western*. It is probable that stories such as "Hell on Wheels" by Alan M. Emley in *Dime Western* (6/34), collected in *Spanish Crossing* (Five Star Westerns, 1998), were stories originally submitted to *Collier's* and declined by the slick magazine. *Collier's*, however, did remain his principal market until 1940. When he returned to Western fiction again in the 1950s, it was to the novel that he returned, and in two cases they were serialized in *The Saturday Evening Post.*

In "Lawman's Debt" Dale Jameson enters his tiny hide-out cabin with $53,740 he has just robbed from the local bank. Dale is the son of a prosperous rancher who has been attracted to a life of plenty through theft. Bat Master's, Dale's boyhood idol and his father's best friend, is the local sheriff, a man now sixty years old. Masters shows up and handcuffs Dale, calling him Brad Kelly, the name by which Jameson has been going in the district. When the dam breaks on their way out of the cañon, Dale feels Masters will go out "honest and clean" and "his one regret was he couldn't go like Bat Masters." Dale saves the sheriff's life in the resulting flood. He could get away at this point, but he signals two riders instead. Masters, who has a broken leg, tells the riders that Brad Kelly was the bank thief and that he drowned. Then he introduces them to Dale Jameson, son of his best friend.

In even the most conventional of LeMay's pulp stories, there is always something that raises them out of the ordinary, be it an image, a character, or a circumstance. In "Death Rides the Trionte" by Alan M. Emley in *Thrilling Western* (3/37), collected in *West of Nowhere*, it is stated that "a cattle king and a cold, ambitious killer was Wade Jeffries. . . ."—but a mysterious gang is making trouble for him. This group turns out to be the landowners who Jeffries drove out and they are now preying on his payrolls and cattle. A masked stranger, dressed in black, rides with them but is not one of them. If this story had a hero, it would be this sinister character, but it does not, nor is there a heroine, or a female character of any kind. At the end, after a terrific shoot-out, the masked rider objects to Wade's peace offer. He is Dan Morgan, his face hideously scarred by the fire that destroyed his family, and he demands a duel with the man behind this heinous crime. Jeffries cheats and shoots Morgan in the back while he is still taking his paces. Before he dies, Morgan is able to do for Jeffries. The sheriff and a posse arrive too late. There is nothing for them to do. The resolution lacks any note of triumph. Any one of these unconventional elements would have been sufficient for this story to be turned down by *Collier's*, but an author could experiment in the pulps in ways impossible in slick magazines.

In "Trail Driver's Luck" in *Collier's* (7/5/30), collected in *The Bells of San Juan*, Cherry Frazee is herding 5,000 head of drought-punished cattle he has bought in old Mexico. "Long chances were his natural roads to fortune, punishment his meat." At the Contrera *rancho*, Cherry encounters again Francisca Contrera, a girl who he once kissed, and learns that a revolt in the district has caused an army to enter the area with the possible threat of his herd's being confiscated. In a desiccated orchard behind the *rancho*, to his own surprise Cherry finds himself clandestinely meeting with Francisca and promising to come back for her so they can marry in three days' time even though she is engaged to another man. If LeMay's pulp stories are more plot-driven than character-driven, the opposite is often the case in those published in *Collier's*. Human nature is unpredictable. Francisca is shocked by this proposal but she asks Cherry to reaffirm the three days. On the trail, trying to get to the U.S. border before his herd is seized, Cherry receives a cryptic message from Francisca that presents him with a dilemma. He realizes that, if he goes back to her now, he will lose the herd, but the note also makes it evident that, if he stays with the herd, he will lose Francisca. Cherry chooses Francisca. He finds her hiding in the deserted *rancho*, with only the old *padre* present. She tricked her father into thinking she headed south with Cherry. The *padre* marries them and they spend their wedding night in Francisca's room. Cherry awakens to the sound of rain. His herd is saved right where he left it, still on Contrera land. Francisca, he acknowledges, is his "luck, luck past all believing."

In "To Save a Girl" in *Collier's* (9/27/30), old Dennis O'Riley (despite his Irish name) claims he's the Dutchman of legend who lost the way to his mine in the 1880s. The time frame is 1930 with automobiles. Wally Parker is a wealthy man who wants to marry O'Riley's granddaughter, June. To accomplish this he knows he will have to end the old man's obsession with his lost mine and he offers Hunter money to help in his scheme. Hunter rejects the offer and then promises June he will help them locate the mine. When they find it, the mystery of just who really is Dennis O'Riley is not solved. "No one could doubt the reality of the tears which the old man tried to hide as they trickled into his beard, nor the overwhelming emotion of June O'Riley as she hugged her grandfather close in her arms." Steve, convinced the mine is a bust, sells his Three Bar for $6,000 and arranges for the assayer to offer this money to June to purchase her share of the claim so at least she will have something. The assay finds the ore is sylvanium, 24% gold, 13% silver. Wally Parker accuses Hunter of fraud for trying to buy out June's share for such a pittance and Steve realizes he has been "a fool who made himself look like a crook." June knows better, however; she knows Steve to be a generous man and is in love with him.

LeMay's Western novels of the 1930s are more conventional in scope and theme than either those from the 1920s or the 1950s. Here, again, he may have been influenced by Ernest Haycox whose first magazine serial was published as *Free Grass* (Doubleday, Doran, 1929) and has as its background conflicts during a cattle drive. Haycox followed this serial with a number of rangeland novels that frequently have an element of mystery as an integral part of the plot, most of them serialized in *Collier's*. LeMay's *Gunsight Trail* (Farrar & Rinehart, 1931) focuses on a range war while *Winter Range* (Farrar & Rinehart, 1932) opens with an inquest and involves the unraveling of the murder of wealthy rancher and banker, John Mason. It was first serialized in *Collier's* in ten installments (12/19/31–2/20/32) and later reprinted in one installment as "Death on the Rimrock" in *Western Fiction* (5/35). It is quite possibly LeMay's finest novel from this decade.

A series of murders that have plagued a rangeland community is at the center of *Cattle Kingdom* (Farrar & Rinehart, 1933). This novel was first serialized in *Collier's* in ten installments (3/4/33–5/6/33) under the title "Cold Trails" and readers of the magazine were told that here was both a Western and a mystery story. *Thunder in the Dust* (Farrar & Rinehart, 1934) is set in Baja California and weaves together plot elements of cattle rustling, murder, and a Mexican revolutionist who recruits an army to overthrow the Mexican government. The basic conflict in *The Smoky Years* (Farrar & Rinehart, 1935) is a struggle for justice. It was serialized in *Collier's* and reprinted in one installment as "Outlaw Cavalcade" in *Western Fiction* (3/36).

As *The Smoky Years* opens, Dusty King and Lew Gordon are going to bid against Ben Thorpe, a crooked cattle magnate, for the Crying Wolf grasslands. Bill Roper, who Dusty King has raised since his father was murdered when he was five, is in love with Jody Gordon, Lew Gordon's only child who is twenty and coming into her own. More than anything else, this is her story, even when she is outside the events being narrated. After Bill kisses her, Jody slaps him so hard the blood runs from his "cut lips." But this violence is only a prelude to her commitment: " 'All yours . . . all, all!' " Jody says. " 'Forever?' " Bill asks. " 'Oh, my darling! Longer than you'll ever be mine. . . .' " Dialogue such as this intimates an inner drama deeper than any suggested by overt events.

Dusty is shot down in Ogallala and this is the pivotal event. Dry Camp Pierce, an outlaw, tells Bill Roper who did it: Cleve Tanner, Walk Lasham, and Ben Thorpe. Bill will take the battle to them even if it means going into league with outlaws. Lew Gordon refuses to condone this action. Jody also breaks with Bill over this decision. They argue and Bill rides off, only for Jody to confront him again on the trail. " 'You're the hardest man I've ever known,' " she tells Roper in her hurt frustration. " 'Nothing could possibly change you. I can see that now. I think you don't care about anything or anybody in the world except this one terrible purpose.'" Yet, having felt this, she comes to regret her own obduracy. Jody tells her father: "'To the last day I live, I'll wish I'd ridden with him then. And now I'll tell you something more. If he ever asks me again, I'll go.'" Marquita, a mixed-blood Indian and Mexican who is Walk Lasham's girl, risks her life to free Roper after he is made captive by Thorpe's henchmen only for her to be slapped down for it. When it is finally only Thorpe and a few of his hardcases, Lew Gordon has a change of heart brought about dramatically when Jody leaves him to join Bill. "'You was right and I was wrong,'" he tells Bill. Lew Gordon is killed in a saloon shoot-out, but so is Ben Thorpe. Bill comes upon Jody later at Dusty King's grave where Bill has notched the wooden cross for Tanner and Lasham. "'In justice,' Jody said, 'in justice, and in memory of courage.' With her own hands she cut the third notch upon the cross, deep and clean."

LeMay wanted nothing more during this period, it would seem, than to be a gentleman rancher with his writing intended to supplement the income generated by raising livestock on his ranch outside Santee, California. Instead, he was plunged into debt after a wet winter disaster wiped out his herd and as a consequence of his divorce. He turned in the late 1930s to screenwriting, early attaching himself to Cecil B. DeMille's unit at Paramount Pictures. LeMay published only one novel in the 1940s, the comic Western, *Useless Cowboy* (Farrar & Rinehart, 1943), adapted for the screen by Nunnally Johnson as *Along Came Jones* (RKO, 1945) in which actor Gary Cooper both played the lead and served as the film's producer. Although LeMay's Hollywood work was scarcely limited to Western films, he did contribute original screen stories for *Trailin' West* (Warner's, 1949), *The Walking Hills* (Columbia, 1949), and *Rocky Mountain* (Warner, 1950) and as early as *North West Mounted Police* (Paramount, 1940) received screen credit for his contribution to a screenplay. LeMay co-produced and adapted *Thunder in the Dust* for the film *The Sundowners* (Eagle-Lion, 1950) and both wrote and directed *High Lonesome* (Eagle-Lion, 1950). However, the finest cinematic achievement based on a LeMay property came with *The Searchers* (Warner, 1956) directed by John Ford and starring John Wayne.

The Searchers is regarded by many as LeMay's masterpiece. Like *The Unforgiven*, it possesses a graphic sense of place; it etches deeply the feats of human endurance that LeMay tended to admire in the American spirit (so clearly foreshadowed in *Painted Ponies* and *The Smoky Years*); and it has that characteristic suggestiveness of tremendous depths and untold stories, often riding on a snatch of dialogue or flashing suddenly in a laconic observation, as when he wrote of Amos Edwards: "Amos was—had always been—in love with his brother's wife." The futility of life hovers here, just as it does in those deep leathery lines carved on the faces of pioneers by the harsh prairies. The fanaticism that drives Bill Roper is a thousand-fold more pronounced in Amos as he embarks on a pursuit that will take him six years and cost him all that is left of his humanity. After her family is brutally murdered by Comanches, Amos's niece, Debbie, is taken captive. Debbie's adopted brother, Mart Pauley, accompanies Amos in the pursuit, but *his* humanity becomes strengthened by the ordeal.

When these two finally find Debbie, the great fear is that her captivity is mental rather than physical. " 'Only—she takes their part now,' " Mart tells Amos. " 'She believes them, not us. Like as if they took out her brain, and put in an Indian brain instead. So that she's an Indian now inside.' " In the context of this story, savagery is not racial in origin, but cultural. What propels the narrative is not wonder at what will happen, what they will find, nor even if they will find it, but the wellsprings of the stubborn hope that drives the protagonists, that will not allow them to surrender, ever, or admit defeat. LeMay said it best in the inscription before the text: "These people had a kind of courage that may be the finest gift of man: the courage of those who simply keep on, and on, doing the next thing, far beyond all reasonable endurance, seldom thinking of themselves as martyred, and never thinking of themselves as brave."

The Unforgiven, as *The Searchers*, served as the basis for a motion picture directed by John Huston and starring Burt Lancaster and Audrey Hepburn. LeMay's dedication is, again, a laconic glimpse into the inner story within the narrative: "To my daughters *Jody* and *Molly,* in the belief that no little girl ever knows how much she is loved." The Dancing Bird is the name given to the grasslands claimed jointly by the Zachary clan and the Rawlins clan. Rachel Zachary, who was orphaned as an infant, was found and adopted by the Zachary clan. She is suspected of having Kiowa blood. After writing so many stories himself with widowers and their young daughters, here LeMay has the Zachary *paterfamilias* the one who is dead and his rôle has been assumed by his eldest son, Ben, who has taken charge of the family consisting of his mother, his two younger brothers, and Rachel. They live in a sod house and make their living raising cattle. Old Zeb Rawlins's wife, Hagar, was once captured and raped by Indians and she still walks with difficulty because her ankles had been tied beneath the horse on which she rode when a prisoner. The Rawlinses have two daughters and two sons.

The two families are mounting a cattle drive when a flare-up of prejudice on account of Rachel causes Ben to withdraw. Abe Kelsey, a vicious squawman, claims his son captured by the Kiowas now goes by the name Seth, and he is reputed to be more vicious than any of the Indians. Again, LeMay makes his point emphatically: behavior comes as a consequence of culture and not race. Rachel is now no more a Kiowa, if indeed she ever was, than Seth is a white man no matter the color of his skin. Moreover, the Kiowas are shown to differ from many other Indian tribes in that they "raided for glory, loot, and sport. . . . The vast areas the Horse Soldier required, in order to live by the hunt, could not much longer be held against a race that fed a thousand people upon the land the Wild Tribes needed to feed one. The buffalo, the one great essential to nomadic life on the prairie, was already going, and would soon be gone."

Ben finally does go on the cattle drive to market, and, while the men are gone, the Kiowas attack. In an earlier scene the Kiowas have been shown in action and so the reader experiences all the terror of such an attack and knows what is meant by total war. In the earlier battle a Kiowa "took the child by the feet and slung him high in the air, into the river. He was hardly more than a baby; didn't know what swimming was, but there under the river he fought for his life. Soon they saw him crawling to the bank, slipping in the wet clay, but making it out of the water. A young savage fitted an arrow, and shot the little struggling fellow in the face. The child went under—yet in a few moments appeared again, floundering and strangling. The arrow had fallen away, but the little face was streaming blood. The bow twanged again, and again the river closed over the child's head. Then, unbelievably, the little boy appeared one more time. One eye socket was empty, but he was trying still. It took another arrow before the child went down to stay, under the muddy water."

The Indian wars, as LeMay had demonstrated as early as *Painted Ponies*, were fought equally against women and children as they were between men on both sides. For the tension and suspense of enduring a determined assault and struggling just to survive it, there are few books as effective and powerful on a visceral level as *The Unforgiven*. Ben and Rachel are united at the end, closer perhaps than brother and sister. Cash Zachary, who was killed in the attack, had made inquiries about Rachel's origin among the Kiowas when relations were less strained between them and an answer was given to him on an animal skin. Ben burns the skin without reading its pictograms. Once more, even though endurance has won the day, the story closes with the impression that for the survivors it was only a Pyrrhic victory accompanied by an incalculable sense of loss that not even time will ever heal.

By Dim and Flaring Lamps is set in the early days of 1861 with much of the action centered around riverboats. Shep Daniels is the principal protagonist. Together with his father and younger brother Trapper, Shep works in his father's business of raising and selling mules. On the eve of a nation about to go to war against itself, the unrealistic demand of the New Englanders rings throughout the border states and into the old South. They "clamored for the turning loose of a million slaves in the Missouri and Mississippi valleys—without any suggestion whatever for their placement, feeding, or control. The plantations would go back to the wilderness, of course, and those hundreds of thousands of chattel field hands would wander homeless, as dangerous as only a helplessly starving horde can be. . . ."

Rodger Ashland, scion of wealthy Tyler Ashland who is the leader of the Missouri militia supporting the secessionists, cousin to Julie DeLorme and in love with her, is also the clandestine head of a gang of renegade long riders preying upon farmers and ranchers in the state. In a most adept and memorable suggestion of far more than is ever to be shown directly, it is recalled that when Rodger was a toddler he was afraid of the dark. Tyler Ashland would have nothing of such nonsense from his son and so he locked him in his room in the dark. Repeatedly the child pleaded for " 'Daddy.' " It was then that Rodger's mother told her husband: " 'All your life . . . and in the hour of your death, you are going to hear that little voice. . . .' " At the end, after Tyler is wounded in a duel with Rodger and Rodger is killed by Shep Daniels (whose father Rodger had murdered), Tyler comments: " 'I have no son . . . I killed him slowly, many years ago.' "

The struggles of a nation dealing with its past and its differences are paralleled in this novel with the struggles of the younger generation with their parents and with the lives they want to lead: Julie with her father and her uncle; Shep and Trapper with their father for whom most of the meaning vanished from his life when their mother died; Rodger and Tyler Ashland with each other. The ending is bittersweet. Courage and endurance are rewarded, but only at a very great price.

Alan LeMay died on April 27, 1964. *By Dim and Flaring Lamps* was his last novel.

LeMay's contribution to the Western story was a substantial one, in the short stories he wrote in the 1920s and 1930s, and especially in his last three novels. Even in his shorter fiction for *Collier's* he could create a graphic sense of place and characters of some depth. In his later novels he provided fastidious reconstructions of what pioneer life was like, peopled with complex characters whose motives are anything but obvious, revealing a psychological dimension of inner voices within the fabric of his narratives. His talent for building suspense and conflict intensified and the images and situations he evoked remain long after his stories are read, inviting and rewarding one in re-reading them, so pervasive and suggestive is the subtlety of his characterizations.

Jon Tuska
Portland, Oregon

Tonopah Range

I

To kill a man in the middle of Moloch's only street, and walk away unseen, was possible under no earthly condition but one—there must be a southeast wind.

Night and day the copper camp swarmed with hard-rock men of the doublejack and drill, and hairy-chested smelter hands who, after a siege of Moloch, could have stoked the jaws of hell itself, and felt at home. They came off shift at all hours, never leaving empty that single street—nor the saloons.

To Moloch, also—especially on Saturday nights—came the riders of the arid Tonopah ranges, lean-hipped men in broad hats, brush jackets, and high-heeled boots. The twin smelter stacks of Moloch thrust 100 feet into the air from the foot of their barren hills, and marked their place by a red flare at night and a mile-high pillar of yellow smoke by day. But you could ride four ways from Moloch for many days without seeing another town, and, when you got a little way off from the smelter town, and looked back, you saw it dwarfed by the mountains behind, reduced by the distances of the desert to a dark speck that flaunted an inconsequential feather. And then you knew that the vast valley of the Tonopah was cattle country yet, and would be for long years to come.

Sometimes the smashing voices of guns spoke in the Moloch street, between the bright-lighted saloons, and almost always there was a score of witnesses to regale the throngs along the bars with the ten-times-told tale of who had fought it out, and why. Yet it was in the middle of Moloch, and on Saturday night, too, that Walt Rathbone died, shot twice through the chest and once through the head. And although 100 heard the shots, and knew them for what they were, there was no witness to the killing.

About once in forty days a southeast wind swept Moloch, a wind that pressed the sulphurous smoke of the smelter downward upon the town's huddle of shanties. Through that dense dry cloud the lights of the saloons shone, dim and quenched, and the coughing, swearing men in the street were vague, moving blurs. Such a southeaster was snoring smoke downward upon Moloch the night Rathbone was killed.

Through the smoke sounded the heavy, blasting *thud* of two shots, then one more. Moloch observed a queer, strained half minute of silence, while everyone listened. Then, gradually at first, men began to move again, and come out of saloons—in the smoke-fogged darkness shouted questions sounded and hurrying feet, for now everyone was curious to know who, if anyone, had been killed.

So dense was the acrid yellow cloud, however, that many minutes were spent in futile blundering about before Lee Sloper, who was not searching at all, stumbled over the fallen man. Sloper and his lanky sidekick, Elmer Law, picked up Walt Rathbone and carried him into the Gun Rack Bar, where they laid him on the floor.

A tall old man, whose broad hat and black neckerchief marked him as one of the few cowmen in the room, choked out an oath so savage that it seemed to strangle in his throat, and stepped away from the bar to drop to one knee beside the dead man and push back an eyelid with huge, gnarled fingers. This man's face seemed to be made up of hard folds of weathered leather, with a broken nose, and a blue three-cornered scar under the left eye, and Sloper instantly knew that he had seen this man before. There were crow's-feet at the corners of the cattleman's eyes, as if that incredibly ugly face could smile, but just now it was turning gray with an emotion that could have been nothing but an almighty blasting rage.

The cattleman stepped back to the bar and tossed off the drink he had left there, then struck the empty whiskey glass down upon the bar with such force that the thick glass shattered. He did not notice, but stood there with his big, knotted hand pressed down, insensate, upon the broken glass.

"There," said the old cattleman, his voice quivering under the weight of his anger, "there lies dead the future of the Tonopah!"

Sloper regarded the dead man curiously—an undistinguished figure in the clothes of a cowman, looking unimportant and commonplace, now that all life was gone from face and limbs, and Sloper was wondering what the old cattleman meant. But now there were other diversions.

A gaunt giant of a miner, who would have kept his mouth shut if he had not been full to the eyes with forty rod was pushing forward to confront Sloper. "And what did you shoot him for?" demanded the giant impassively.

Lee Sloper unhurriedly looked over the man he had carried in, making note of certain details for future reference. Just as unhurriedly he looked over the miner, and saw that he was smoky drunk. He turned away.

The Gun Rack was filling rapidly, and a growling yammer of unanswered questions was increasing every minute.

A tall man, very lean and worn-looking, came pushing through the crowd. "Who done this here?" he demanded sharply.

"He did," said the big miner, jerking a thumb at Sloper.

"Jee-rusalem, feller!" said the lean man without heat. He showed Sloper a deputy's badge in his cupped hand. "You sure tipped over the bottle this trip! You know who that is? That's Walt Rathbone, one of the best-known cattlemen around here! You must have known all that, though."

"Never saw him before in my life," said Sloper.

Slowly the deputy let his eyes travel over Lee Sloper, studying the cowboy's angular, homely face with its slightly crooked nose, muscled cheek bones, and hard, shaven jaws, and finally met squarely Sloper's frosty gray eyes. Sloper was a big man, but his long legs gave him a light, balanced look not to be associated with docile or sheep-like ways of doing business.

"You better come right along here with me," said the deputy with some concern. "Fella, you ain't safe. Someone of the Crazy K riders is apt to come busting in here any minute. You better let me slip you in the calaboose, while we get this here straightened out."

"He never done it!" yelped the lanky Elmer Law at Sloper's elbow. "I'll take a smash at the *hombre* that says . . ."

"And who might you be?" demanded the deputy wearily. The crowd was close about them now, the front ranks silent and listening, those in the rear sustaining a clamor of inquiry.

"That's Mister Elmer Law from Nebraska," Sloper supplied. "He isn't very smart."

"And this," Law retorted, "is Bad Lee Sloper . . . he hit a man in Tailholt, Missouri and pretty near knocked him down. By golly, Missouri, I'll learn you to make a fool of me!"

"Seems like you're trying to make this business look funny," the deputy said slowly.

"We're game to get just as funny as you do," said Elmer Law.

The deputy's neck reddened as he glanced quickly over Elmer Law, taking in the lean man's angry, bulging eyes of washed-out blue, his sandy straggle of mustache set slightly crooked, and the dusty folds of the black handkerchief at his neck.

"Don't mind him," drawled Sloper. "He's had some bad falls in the rocks, and it's took a certain effect, but he's good-hearted. Now, I'll tell you this, Mister Deputy. If I'd had reason to shoot this man, I'd have shot him. You don't know me, and I don't know you, and as far as I'm concerned I don't give a hoot. It's your move."

"What's your brand?" asked the deputy.

"Brand? Him branded?" said Elmer Law. "Hell, man, he ain't even been throwed!"

"Shut up, Elmer. We just rode in, mister, from off up behind the Mogollon Rim. Nobody knows us here."

"That settles it," said the deputy shortly, shifting his weight and half turning to leave. "Come on, both of you."

"Where to?" asked Sloper, making no move.

"The calaboose . . . if," the deputy added under his breath, "we can get to it."

"What manner of calaboose do you run, that's so hard to get into?"

"It has four-foot adobe walls, with gun loops," was the laconic answer. "Are you coming or not?"

"Not," said Sloper.

The deputy stepped close, shoved a worried face close to Sloper's ear, and whispered from the corner of his mouth. "You damn' fool, look around you."

"I have," said Sloper, leaning his elbows on the bar behind him.

He did not have to look again to read, or to remember, the massed ring of the red-eyed sulphur men, the shaveless grim visages of the doublejackers—hard-toiling, hard-drinking men, the monotony of whose lives was broken only by their own ready truculence. All those whose attention had been drawn to the Gun Rack Bar were in it now, and knew what was going on, and the crowd mutter was silent. The mob filled the bar, waiting and motionless, except for the weaving of an occasional fast drinker who swayed on his feet, leaning forward as he strove to focus smoldering eyes.

And all through the silence of that crowded room was a deadly, ragged feel of tension, a sense of electric charge that emanated almost visibly from the cleared space before Missouri Sloper, where lay the finished body of Walt Rathbone. It was true that most of those hard-rock men thought lightly and unsentimentally of human life. But a man was dead, and there was a red trickle on the floor, and inevitably the crowd was turned strained and ugly, like steers that smell blood.

The deputy was talking in whispers, but so silent was the room that the nearer rank must certainly have heard.

"I'm telling you, feller, if you're a stranger, you don't know what you're up against here. I don't say you shot him . . . but you've worked your way into a hot spot, that's all. I'd as lief be a shoat in a bear den as to give a Moloch mob an excuse to take *me* apart. They haven't any sense, and they . . ."

"I can see that," said Sloper coolly. "This is all crazy business."

"This is a crazy town," the deputy agreed. "I been here since Moloch struck, and I tell you, you get this town half lit, and it'll stampede over a man like a herd in a thunderstorm. You know what'll happen if one man in the back yells lynch?"

Suddenly his glance snapped over his shoulder to the door.

The heavy front doors of the saloon were swinging shut. They jammed, and were rammed into place by willing shoulders. A bolt shot, and a key grated as it was jerked out of its lock at the back of the room, a padlock clicked.

"Oh, hell a-whistlin'," said the deputy softly. He

licked dry lips, and Sloper saw that the corners of the man's mouth were turning green. "There you are. You asked for it, and you got it."

"And I like it," said Sloper mechanically.

"Great holy cow," moaned Elmer Law. "They've locked the doors. If you think your devil's luck is ever going to get us out of this . . ."

"For Pete's sake, Napper," the deputy whispered to the bartender, "gimme that sawn-off shotgun."

The fat bartender had turned a pasty white. He was gripping the rear edge of the bar, and his eyes were starting from his head.

"Keep your hands where they is!" a voice ordered him.

"I . . . I can't reach it," Napper murmured to the deputy.

The deputy started around the bar.

"Stand still," said a bearded man. The deputy's hands jerked over his head as the muzzle of a gun prodded into his back.

All over the room began a snarl of voices and a shift of feet. "Where's a rope?"

"Git his guns!"

"Watch out for the other!"

"Lock the doors!"

"They're locked all right!"

"Ain't you afraid," said Sloper's hard drawl, "that some of you-all are going to want to get out of here in a minute?"

There was an instant's quiet, followed by a new

angry rumble of voices. The throng swayed and shoved, those behind demanding action, those in front hesitant to draw guns or step across the body of Rathbone, for although Sloper wore but one weapon, it was close under his drooping right hand.

"We're just lynched to hell, Missouri," said Elmer Law in his ear. "Shoot the lights and . . ."

"Lights, hell. There won't be time. Get ready to jump the bar. We'll fight it from behind the . . ."

The big cattleman with the ugly, weathered face had not moved, or spoken, but now, unexpectedly, he stepped into the middle of the situation with both feet.

"You listen to me!" His voice was not exactly a roar; it was deliberate and slow, but it was strong enough and overbearing enough to carry against the rising rumble of confusion, and they listened to what he said. "You listen to me, all of you. You don't know this man. You don't know him, huh? But, by heaven, you know me, I think! Do you know me, huh?"

They knew him all right. The nearest ones of that shoving crowd had been jostling against him, which may have been what set him off in part. But now they drew back, becoming suddenly aware of his presence, and who he was, and in a moment there was a bigger cleared ring around the big, battered old cowman than there was around Lee Sloper and the cattleman that lay dead on the floor.

Sloper let a faint grin twist his mouth. In the back of the crowd in the Gun Rack he had sighted three or four ten-gallon hats, marking where cowboys mingled with the men of the town. At first, when the old cowman had begun speaking his piece, Sloper had thought that it was a stand-off of the range against the town. He now saw that it was not; it was the reckless bluff of one man against a mob, one man alone.

"Clear back from that door!" The ugly, leathery old face was no longer livid with the anger that Missouri Sloper had seen upon it a few moments before. A momentary gleam of slow, grim relish had come into it now, but at the same time it was bitter hard. "Yeah, that's right . . . step on each other's feet! You, Shorty, throw free that bolt . . . quick now! Uhn-huh. That's better."

Now that the crowd had cleared back, Lee Sloper noticed a peculiar thing about the old cowman. Up back of the Mogollon Rim, where Sloper and the lanky Elmer Law had come from, it was good etiquette to wear one gun—a fellow might want to shoot a coyote, or something like that. But it was a long time since Sloper had seen a man who wore two guns. He was looking at one now.

The leather-faced cowman had hooked his elbows on the bar, as had Sloper and Law. His fingers trailed downward casually relaxed—but open, and inconspicuously ready. And just below those gnarled, broken-nailed fingers the black gun butts showed. The old warrior wore no gun belt. The holsters of the paired Colts were concealed inside the legs of his dark-blue pants, so that just the butts showed from the front pockets. It was a peculiar place for guns, since it must have made it difficult for the wearer to sit down, but it made them as inconspicuous as a pair of extremely handy guns could be.

That twinned artillery could mean but one of two things—that the toter was on a fool war strut, which, in view of the cowman's advanced age, did not seem likely, or that he was a man who had acquired more than one set of open and serious-minded enemies.

Slowly the big gnarled hands moved until they rested lightly on their owner's belt, with just the fingertips touching the butts of that unusual number of guns. It was a casual attitude yet, although even readier than before.

"All right, boys," said the old man. Although he did not look at Sloper and Law, everyone somehow knew to whom he spoke. "I guess you recognize that this ain't no place for white men. Go ahead. I'll meet you out in front."

Nonchalantly, with a hundred eyes boring into their backs, Sloper and Law walked outside into the acrid swirl of the smoke.

"Come on! The horses!" Law urged, gripping Sloper's arm. "Child, that was a close one! All I want is to put this smoke pot of a town five thousand miles behind!"

"Wait," said Sloper. "I believe we're going to like this town, Elmer."

"*Like* it?"

"It's got a man in it, Elmer. That's more than lots of towns can say." He moved into the shadows and leaned himself, relaxed and casual, against a post. Slowly and meticulously he began the rolling of a cigarette.

II

"You mean to say," demanded Elmer, regaining his voice, "you ain't got *enough* of this murderous hell smudge of a . . ."

"I want to find out who that old he-wolf is," Missouri Sloper told him.

"I'm willing to inquire in the next town," said Elmer Law. "I scare awful easy, Missouri, and I've seen enough."

"You should have thought of that when you were begging for trouble in there."

"I lost my temper," Elmer admitted. "But I ain't mad any more . . . and this place is full of crazy people."

" 'There lies dead,' " Missouri quoted softly, " 'the future of the Tonopah.' "

"You gone nuts, too?"

"I was just wondering about something."

The old cattleman of the two guns now joined them, sidling casually out of the bar. His mildly interested gaze remained fixed within the saloon until he was entirely out of line with the door. Then he turned and came, slowly still, to where Sloper waited. He was cursing under his breath in bitter, measured oaths.

"For twenty years," said the two-gunner, apparently talking more to himself than to Sloper, "for twenty long years I've fought for the Tonopah water, and give all the last part of my life to one thing. And now, a couple of shots in the sulphur smoke, and all that's gone, and the water under Tonopah's as good as lost forever." They could not see his face, but by the quiver of anger in his voice they could picture it as they had seen it before, when the tall old man had straightened up from examining the dead rancher.

"What's he talking about?" whispered Elmer in Sloper's ear. "I think he's crazy, too. Let's git out o' here, Missouri."

In the Gun Rack Bar an excited rumble had broken out again, as the old cattleman withdrew, the growl of voices punctuated here and there by drunkenly angry yells.

"They're telling each other what they was about to do," said the big man contemptuously, turning his attention for a moment to the saloon. "The longer I live, the lower opinion I got of the human race. Let's just step aside here a minute, fellers."

He waited, his gaze on the barroom door. He was not kept waiting long. A bulge of men came pushing onto the wooden sidewalk, those in front more or less tentative of movement, but propelled by the enthusiasm of those behind. The old man's right-hand gun crashed, splintering the boards at their feet.

"Git back there!" he bellowed. The crowd went tumbling back.

"I'd rather be dead," said the old misanthrope, "than be the average man." The two walked with him as he turned and strode, unhurriedly, down the walk.

"Mister," said Missouri Sloper, "my partner and I want you to know we sure appreciate the interest you took in our little embarrassment back there, and we like your guts."

"Guts didn't enter in," the cowman grumbled. "A two-year-old kid can stand off the average mob with his candy stick. They make me plenty sick."

"This here is Elmer Law," said Sloper. "Just an average man, like you was speaking about."

"And this," snapped Elmer, "is Missouri Sloper, what pulled our average down."

"Sloper," said the old cowman. "I place you now. Yes, I knew I'd seen you some place. Up at Flagstaff, it was, and you was loading beef for Bob MacIntyre . . . one of the best friends I ever had."

"That makes you Gideon Holt," said Sloper instantly.

He remembered the occasion upon which he had seen Holt now. Curious that he should have forgotten, for it had been upon one of the big days of Sloper's life—the day that old Bob MacIntyre had made him foreman of the Bar C. Foreman of the vast Bar C at the age of twenty-two, and, although he had continued in that capacity for the four years since, Sloper had never understood why he had been placed in charge of so many older and—as far as he could see—much better cowboys.

"Yep, Holt's my name. Horntoad Holt, they call me, the idea being to offer an insult to the toad. How long did you last as foreman for Bob MacIntyre?"

"Ever since."

"And then?" Holt asked curiously.

"I heard the name Tonopah every once in a while, and last month I got to wondering what the Tonopah might look like, so I quit. Just a born saddle bum, I expect, Mister Holt."

Holt grunted, his mind elsewhere. "Tonopah," he repeated slowly, as if the word were unfamiliar. "You wondered what it was. Me, I'm wondering what it *might* have been. Tonopah water . . ." Suddenly that almighty wrath of his swept him again, choking his voice down to a grating snarl. "The Tonopah water lost out, right here in this street tonight. But so help me, if it's war they want, it's war they get! I've spent the last third of my life fighting to give the Tonopah water, and I don't know how many years I have left. But I'll give the last of my life, and the last year, and the last day to paying that outfit back, and, if all hell doesn't rise up and smoke in the Tonopah, from here out . . ." He checked himself suddenly. Then he turned and extended his hand. "Well, so long, fellers," he said in a dead voice. "Glad to have been there when you talked up to that trash in the bar."

"We're looking for jobs, Mister Holt," said Missouri, "and, if you have anything open . . ."

"You mean," said Holt slowly, "you want jobs with me?"

"Wa-it a minute," said Elmer Law—but under his breath.

"I don't know what it's about, this ruction here," said Sloper, "but I've heard MacIntyre speak of you often enough to guess I'd just as lief swing your side."

"Gunfighter, by any chance?"

"No, sir."

"Well, I can't hardly refuse a foreman off of Bob MacIntyre's with good men so scarce. I don't guess you know what you're heading into, though, either. Well, I'll tell you, Sloper . . . you can have jobs, if you want 'em . . . and, when you don't want 'em, I guess you can quit."

"Elmer, we've found work."

"Work?" said Elmer faintly.

"Right now," said Holt, "you boys better ride on out to my ranch. You got ponies here? It's twenty mile, but the first ten of it before you bed down will make you a whole heap safer. Me, I've got to find out a few things . . . like where was Walt Rathbone last seen. You take the downcountry trail to the forks and . . ."

"A left-handed man," said Missouri, "who smokes a pipe will he able to tell you . . . but I suppose you noticed all that."

"What's this? A left-handed . . . what are you talking about?"

"Why, I'm thinking of that fresh splinter stab in Walt Rathbone's left forefinger."

"I didn't look that close. What about it""

"Rathbone was left-handed . . . his gun was on that side. On the side of his left forefinger I saw a little torn stab in the skin, new and fresh, like you might make running your hand onto a splinter pretty hard. Now you take a man who knew this town pretty well, and was left-handed, too, and, if by chance that man smoked a pipe . . ."

"By gum, you're absolutely right," said Holt. He thought for a moment. "Come in here!"

He led the way into another bar—called the Horse's Neck—where stood a sallow and melancholy man, who polished his bar top with a dirty rag held in his left hand.

"You know," said Missouri to the bartender, "there ought to be a law making people sandpaper the edges of tables. I was striking a match, just now, and I rammed a splinter into my knuckle darned near through to the bone."

"Ain't it the truth?" said the bartender. "I was up at the smelter office one day, talking to Mort Six, and I struck a match under the table and run a splinter in my finger about three inches long . . ."

Holt slammed his fist on the bar, and started for the door. "That was a good short cut, Sloper," he said when they were in the street. "I forgot Walt smoked a pipe. A pipe keeps going out so much that just about everything in the world has had a match struck on it by a pipe smoker."

"And there's no other way," agreed Elmer Law, "that you can stick your finger quite so hard as when you take a table with a splintery edge, and take a match . . ."

Through the smoke at the head of the street loomed the mighty twin stacks of the Moloch smelter, black columns forever topped with flowers of flame. Old Gideon Holt strode through the sulphurous smother of the smoke to a small building of sheet iron and unpainted wood, and thrust open the door.

Morton Six, owner and principal operator of the Moloch smelter, was, at first sight, a man of most commonplace appearance. Middle-aged, middle height, middle coloring—he was in no way a conspicuous figure. Yet, as he raised tired gray eyes from a sheet of computations on the table before him, something of the force of the man was apparent in his gaze. A man does not make himself lord of even so limited a principality as the smelter of Moloch without having within him certain strengths of will, intelligence, and endurance—and a certain rapacity.

There was little to indicate rapacity, however, in the tired eyes of Morton Six. His gaze was frank and direct, and rather more than usually open. He smiled—wearily—as the three pushed into his office, and withdrew his hand from a drawer at his side. "I guess I can put away my gun," he said frankly. "You don't deal with several hundred hard-rock men without making an enemy here and there . . . and you never know who is coming through a door."

"Mort Six," said Holt, "what time did Walt Rathbone leave this room?"

"About seven o'clock," said Mort Six. "He was here for just a few minutes after dinner." He rested his head on his hand, his fingers in his rumpled hair, and steadily returned old Holt's stare. Then gradually his face hardened under the truculent gaze of the cattleman. "Why?" he demanded less amiably.

Holt looked questioningly at Missouri Sloper.

"It's half past eight," said Sloper, glancing at the clock on the wall.

"Eight twenty-three," Morton Six corrected him.

Elmer Law consulted his watch. "That clock is exactly six and three-quarter minutes fast," he stated. "I set my watch at the White Front Hotel, just tonight."

"The hotel clock is slow . . . out of order," said Six.

"Be that as it may," Sloper said, "that splinter mark was a whole lot less than an hour old. There was a little small drop of blood on it yet."

"You want to change your statement about what time Walt Rathbone left here?" Holt asked Six.

"Why?" said Six again, sitting up.

The brown-paper cigarette Holt smoked was dead between his lips. He sat down opposite Morton Six at the table, and took a match from his pocket. "Walt Rathbone is dead," he said.

The chair under Morton Six tipped over backwards as the smelter man jerked to his feet. "What?"

"But you knew that maybe?" Holt suggested, unmoved.

"Was that what that shooting was?"

"You heard it, then?"

"I naturally heard shots. Who did it?"

"Persons unknown," grunted Holt. "Mort Six," he went on softly, "you know me. I speak straight out . . . and I back my play. What motive might you have for wanting Walt Rathbone dead?"

Six looked at the rancher for a moment before he jerked out a dry chuckle. "Enough," he said, and sat down abruptly.

"You admit that."

"Admit . . . hell, I stated it."

"You and me have been considerable opposed," said Holt, his eyes hard on Mort Six's face.

"Well, you might say so," agreed Six with another unpleasant chuckle. "If it hadn't been for your damned bullheadedness, by this time I'd have made the Three Brand property a paying thing for us all."

"That's as may be," said Holt. "As you know, I've done all I could to keep my two partners in the Three Brand discovery from selling out. You know what I wanted. I wanted to turn the profits of the Three Brand copper ledges into water for the valley of the Tonopah, and make it a real cow country at last. And you know I've done all in my power to keep Dundee and Rathbone from selling out on me. And . . ."

"If you and Rathbone had half the sense of Dundee," said Six ill-humoredly, "the Three Brand copper would be doing you some good by now."

"I'm coming to that. Dundee has held like a bulldog to the idea of selling outright. I held out for development and water. Walt, he's always wavered. And Dundee and I have felt pretty bitter on the subject, keeping all that ore unexploited because we owned equal shares and couldn't get together. Al-mighty bitter. And yet"—he leveled the unlit match at Six like a tiny gun, and his voice grated—"there's never been one word of talk about fight, or feud . . . except by those outside the deal. And now . . ."

"Well, there's been plenty of talk outside," said Six.

"Oh, it's been strained enough," Holt admitted. "But now you look here. You've been on the inside of this thing as much as anybody except Dundee, Rathbone, and me. You've been at the bottom of the trouble against me . . . you egging on Dundee to sell to you, you knocking the water project with your phony engineering, you flashing greenbacks in the eyes of Rathbone and Dundee. I've stood plenty from you, along those lines, Mort."

"Someday, when I withdraw my offers, you'll wish you'd took me," growled Six. "And get this, I will withdraw, one of these days. You don't know what's good for you."

"I've stood a lot," Holt pushed on, not seeming to hear him. "But now the time has come when Rathbone is dead . . . murdered . . . and it's necessary to find his killer. And I'll tell you here and now, before these witnesses, if you think you're going to hold out information on me and live through it . . ."

"I told you frankly enough Rathbone was here, and I told you what time," broke in Six harshly.

"And you told me a damned lie!" Holt thundered.

There was a short silence between them, and the roar of the smelter bore heavily upon the ears of the cowmen, whose ears were attuned to open distances and the winds.

"Just what do you mean by that?" Six demanded at last, his voice so low it was almost lost under the muffled growl of the smelter.

"If you want to know what you're up against," said Holt slowly, "I'll tell you a few things that happened in this room tonight. Just before Rathbone left this place, for example, he lit his pipe. He struck his match on the under side of the table edge. At the moment, he was kind of mad, and it made his hands quicker. He ripped the match hard along the wood, with his left hand. Then he got up and went out."

A queer expression came into Mort Six's face. It was plain that he was rocked back on his heels by this description. His eyes shot to the single small window, the panes of which were thickly painted over with white paint, then over his shoulder to a door behind him—but this was heavy, solid, and padlocked shut.

"That's all true," he admitted. "And where the hell were *you* spying from, Holt?"

"You want to know how I know?" said Holt without triumph. "I know because he stuck his finger on a splinter in the table's edge . . . like this!"

He ripped his match along the underside of the table, but as his hand came up they saw an expression of faint puzzlement cross his face.

"Now wait a minute," said Six, examining his edge of the table. "There's no splinters in this table. The last table I had I splintered my finger on more than once. But that burned when this shack burned, two months ago."

"No," admitted Holt, "damned if there's any splinters on this side, either."

Six laughed nastily. "You called me a liar a minute ago."

"I take it back," said Holt slowly, meeting his eye.

"You'll do better than that . . . you'll apologize!"

"All right . . . I apologize." Holt's voice was low and dead, as if his mind were elsewhere altogether. And his eyes were running all around the little room, so that Missouri Sloper knew that Holt was looking for some other place where a match could have been struck—some place where a man could run a splinter into his hand.

"Rathbone had a splinter in his finger, did he?" said Six.

That was not bad, thought Sloper; Six had brains, he guessed, to unravel their line of reasoning so quickly, almost at a glance. Missouri was keeping his attention on the right hand of Mort Six, remembering that gun in the drawer by the smelter man's side.

"A fine piece of evidence that would have been," Six went on. "Figure to hang a man on a splinter, Holt? I guess you don't know much about evidence, Holt, and the law."

"When I get the truth," said Holt, "I'll see that the score is evened up, all right. I'm not worrying about evidence before the law." His voice was even and cold. "When a man's old, he can afford to spend himself like a bullet out of a gun, and what comes after that doesn't make much difference any more, to him or anyone else." He brought his eyes sharply back to Mort Six. "You had reason enough to kill him, you say. Tired of his everlasting wavering about our selling the Three Brand lode to you?"

Morton Six hesitated for only the fraction of a moment. "He wasn't wavering any more, Holt."

"You mean?"

"You know I've always wanted the Three Brand lode. Twenty times I've offered you three a good price. If I could have persuaded Rathbone to sell, Rathbone and Dundee could have overridden you, two against one in the shares, and sold to me. Tonight I made Rathbone a final offer. He refused."

"Are you trying to tell me he refused to swing with Dundee . . . to sell?"

"Once and for all, he said, his answer was no, and he was going over to your side of the fence.

'Come on with the Tonopah water!' Those were his last words before he left here."

Holt snarled out a bitter oath. "And his last words on earth, I've got no doubt."

"I think not. He was gone from here more than an hour before I heard those shots that you say ended him."

"To think how close the Tonopah come to getting its water." The gray rage was coming into Holt's face again.

"It's true that he left here pretty mad," Six concluded. "It's also true that I was pretty sore myself, and I'm not wasting any sentiment on him now. I'm sick and tired of the bullheadedness that stands in the way of that development and . . ."

"That stands in the way of getting these mountains, and leaving the country barren and stripped," amended Holt, his eyes flaring for a moment.

"And I'll tell you this," Six finished. "Rathbone's death reopens the whole question of who is to develop the Three Brand copper lode. And"—an intensity, almost a note of exultation, came into his eyes, his voice—"I doubt if all hell can stop me now from gathering in the Three Brand lode."

As those two faced each other across the table in the little room that was forever filled with the ceaseless muffled roar of the smelter Mort Six had built, Sloper saw that Six, the younger man, was the one who held back a triumphant and ruthless energy, and that Gideon Holt looked stripped, beaten, and old. The energy of the man who wrung wealth from the mountains almost visibly arced out at the hard old man of the wasted plains. Yet—in Gideon Holt was a granite-like quality such that Sloper was somehow reminded by that clash of wills of waves breaking futilely at the foot of a great rock.

"I'll be deep under the ground when you do," Holt told Morton Six with heavy finality.

"The sooner the better," Six answered.

"But," said Holt, "there'll be others with me, and before me."

"Is that a threat?"

"It's a prophecy."

Missouri Sloper and Elmer Law followed as the old man stumped out.

"He stood his ground pretty good," said Sloper, when they were in the street again.

"Yes . . . we held no cards against him," admitted Holt.

"I suppose it's no use looking for any more splinters. There's a million splinters in the world . . . some pretty near everywhere that there's a piece of wood."

"That's true. It was just a chance of reconstructing a little scene, and maybe surprising Six into showing his hand. But . . . the last thing I expected was that he would be so plain open about the whole business."

"It isn't like him, then?" Missouri asked.

"Oh, I've always found him straightforward enough. But, in this case . . . we'll just have to look further, that's all. I'll stay in town over tomorrow and see what I can find out. Gosh, I wish I could find Art Humphreys. He's the only one of my riders in town tonight. Oh, well. . . ."

"Rathbone had to be some place in that hour," said Elmer Law. "It stands to reason."

"If anybody knows where he was, I'll find out . . . that is, if anybody but Mort Six knows. It's pretty plain we're not going to get anything more out of him. Meantime . . . there's something you boys can do for me . . . not as hired hands, but as a favor, if you want. I'd like for you to ride out to Dundee's ranch . . . the Bar Five . . . and tell him about Walt Rathbone being shot."

"Sure," said Missouri. "Shall we say we came from you?"

"Naturally." Suddenly a different angle seemed to strike old Holt. "No! Avoid that subject. Tell him the truth if he asks. But . . . as for working for me, you ain't. Get that?"

"But you hired us on, didn't you?" said Elmer Law.

"You're hereby fired. Maybe when you've talked to Dundee, you won't want any jobs with me. Maybe you'd rather work for him. In fact, you might ride out there and ask him for work . . . you won't get it, though. After that, if you still want to work for me, I'll see what's open."

"If this is a spying job, Mister Holt, I . . . ," began Missouri.

"Did I say that?"

"You just want us to tell him, and see how he takes it? Then come back and tell you?"

"I know how he'll take it. And for that matter you don't even need to come back, if you don't want. He has to be informed, that's all. Tell him the truth, and, if he asks if I sent you, say I did. If you don't want to do that, I can . . ."

"We'll do that, Mister Holt."

"I'll give you fresh ponies from some I have in the livery corral. It's better'n thirty miles. You better sleep on the trail."

"On our way!"

III

The sun was low behind the dark ranges that hemmed the valley of the Tonopah when Sloper and Elmer Law at last approached the adobe ranch buildings of the Bar Five, lonely upon the face of the desert.

An old man, who Sloper correctly assumed to be Andry Dundee himself, walked out to meet them, and Elmer and Missouri exchanged a brief glance as they saw that Dundee carried a rifle in the crook of his arm negligently, as if it were an accustomed part of his apparel.

"This," said Lee Sloper apologetically, "is Mister Law. He's trying to learn the cowboy business, since they got him to leave Nebraska."

"And this," said Elmer Law in turn, "is Lee Sloper. He once led a large party of Missourians into the West. They turned back, though, when they see he'd made it safely to the state line."

"Pleased to meetcha," said Andry Dundee without visible delight. He let the somber smolder of his deep-set eyes play briefly upon Elmer Law, then, more slowly, over Lee Sloper.

Dundee's wiry mustache was the color of steel, but the stubble that salted his gaunt jaws was silver, and only a scant fringe of hair moderated his baldness. His buckskin gloves, turned down over his hands because of the heat, exposed wrists strong-boned and sharp-corded.

"I'll be obliged," he said, "if you'll step down and have somethin' to eat. We're just about to draw up."

Elmer Law swung down with agility. "Why, to be frank, Mister Dundee, your kind invite pulls me out of a bad hole. I don't eat no more than a bird does myself, but the fact is I haven't been able to rake up anything for Missouri since about noon, and he's hog hungry. A hard man to keep fed, Missouri is, and very frequently . . ."

Missouri Sloper swung down slowly, almost as if he had stiffened in the saddle, which, of course, was not possible. A sudden hesitancy had taken an unconscious effect upon him. Just as Law and Sloper had pulled up in front of the ranch house, another rider had galloped in from another direction and this rider was a girl.

Past the corner of the long, flat-topped adobe ranch house Missouri could see the corral, set among some pepper trees fifty yards beyond. While old Andry Dundee walked slowly out to speak to them, Sloper had watched the girl come in, light and careless in the saddle of a palomino horse, her hair wind-blown, and something had turned over inside of Missouri Sloper. He thought to himself: *That's right pretty.* He had no fitting words to express what he knew was so—that brief picture of the girl on the pale, silver-tailed horse had in it the elements of all beauty, all loveliness. It was the sort of thing riders sing about mournfully on night circle, to the words and tune of "Bill Morgan's Knee" or "Twenty Miles from Carson in the Rain". There was something hurtful in anything so pretty as that. But a certain caginess followed his first long-range shock of admiration. Experience told Missouri that a close-up was liable to be almighty disappointing in a case like that, and instinctively he shied off from disillusionment. All other things equal, he would have ridden on, keeping that one untested glimpse of heaven to sing about on long saddle nights with the cows.

"How's the year?" Missouri asked, as they

walked up to the ranch house. He was noticing the ancient four-foot-thick walls of the adobe building, the hand-hewn doors, and jutting out of the adobe near the wall tops the rough, crooked butts of the logs that supported the flat roof. It was a Southwestern type of construction that the Spaniards had learned from the Pueblos long ago. Built to last forever. Built without forethought of such innovations as running water, or efficient heat and light, which the future might hold.

"We've had a pretty good year," Dundee told him. "Yes, sir, the stock is looking just about as good as I ever saw it."

Considering the gaunt, undersized scrub herds that Missouri Sloper had noticed during the ride from Moloch—stock starved by the desert and gaunted by lack of water—Sloper was astonished at Dundee's answer. He kept a pokerface, however.

"How many head you carrying to the section in these parts, Mister Dundee?"

"The range will carry ten head to the section," said Dundee almost defiantly. "But we're only running eight, so's not to overgraze."

Ten head to graze 640 acres! On the dry Staked Plains, Sloper recalled, they often carried twenty-two, and in the rimrock country sometimes as high as thirty, while Wyoming and Montana men thought both those countries hopeless desert. Sloper wondered why Holt had urged him to remember that Dundee was an able and prosperous rancher—one of the most successful in the Tonopah.

"Gail," said old Dundee, "I want you to meet a couple of people, stopping by here."

Missouri looked up—and remained looking, forgetful of what he was about. For once in his life he was spared disillusion. Gail Dundee was tanned as a biscuit, with hair and eyes the brown of desert grass. Her hair was shorter than it had looked when it was blowing in the wind, but it was loose, and kind of half curly about her neck. It had glints of gold in it, and there were golden glints in her eyes, like the sun getting into shadowed mountain water. She was slender, but it was a slenderness of soft rounded lines, and she walked with the graceful ease of a panther. Sloper was crumpled, as if he had taken a good sock between the eyes.

"I don't know what to say exactly," he said lamely, "except that this sure is unexpected."

"Didn't know I had a daughter?" suggested Dundee suspiciously.

"Well, yes, I heard you had, but I . . ."

"But you thought, after seein' her paw, she'd look like a cross between a chink cook and a mud fence, huh? But she don't take after me, does she?"

"No, sir, she certainly don't. Well . . . that is to say, there is quite a resemblance around the . . . a kind of general resemblance."

"Will you shut your mouth till we've et?" whispered Elmer Law furiously.

"You talk as if you were pointing up stock for purchase," said the girl frostily.

Elmer stepped into the breach. "Don't mind Missouri, folks. He's all right around stock, but you get him out in society and he's just a blanket buck that's lost track of where's his reservation. Like yesterday, when we rode into Moloch. We had drag-tailed across the Mogollon, and dropped down over Hell-a-Mile Pass, and finally made Moloch, after some groping around in the smoke. It was sure smoky . . . you had to cut a hole in the air with an axe in order to spit. And right after we et . . ."

"Supper's getting cold," put in Gail Dundee.

"We was walking down the street," continued Elmer, "as near as we could tell, in all that smoke, which was more like a snootful of cactus than any natural smoke, and put me in mind of a . . ."

"Yes, it gets bad there, with a southeast wind," agreed old Dundee. "Now, if you'll just pull up chairs . . . Lou Stam ain't back, but we won't wait."

"And we was walking along," Elmer went on, "when what does Missouri do but stumble over . . . yes, thankee, I will, I'm a great admirer of warmed-up taters . . . when Missouri stumbles over a . . ."

"Mister Sloper, please, sir," said Gail Dundee

plaintively, "do you have to kick me in the ankle?"

Missouri reddened and choked. "I . . . I thought I was kicking Elmer Law . . . honest I did."

"And for why should you kick poor Elmer Law?" Elmer demanded with his mouth full. "Darned if you ain't outright offensive."

"Yes," agreed Dundee genially, "have some hominy. And while the question's up, what is the sense of kicking people, Sloper?"

"Why, nothing, Mister Dundee, sir," floundered Missouri. "He was about to bring up something not suitable for eating purposes, was all."

"I was no such a thing," said Elmer, bristling. "All I was going to tell was, when Missouri stumbled over this corpse . . ."

"Let be, you fool," said Missouri lethally. Elmer fell into a disgruntled silence, and devoted himself to his food.

The father and daughter exchanged glances.

Dundee said softly: "So there's been another killing, has there?"

"Yes, there has," said Sloper. "I knew you'd likely be interested, but I'm right sorry my talkative friend brought it up at the table. I apologize for him."

"Who was it?" asked Dundee. His voice was slow and quiet, but sharp as lye.

"A rancher named Rathbone."

"*Walt* Rathbone? Of the Crazy K?" Dundee almost whispered after a moment of silence.

"Yes, that was the name I was told, sir."

"Know who done it?" Dundee asked in a queer, half-strangled voice.

"No, sir, that isn't known, I think. We heard shots, there in the street, about eight o'clock in the evening. They were nearby, but what with the smoke I couldn't tell exactly where they were from, and right after that there were fellers hunting around the smoke to find out what happened. And it just happened it was me run across the man that was shot, and Elmer and I picked him up and carried him into the Gun Rack Bar. His gun was in his holster, as he lay. He'd been shot three times, and he was dead."

Dundee sat back, his plate untouched, and loaded his pipe. The veins stood out on his forehead, and his eyes glowed with the brassy light of the night sky above the smelters of Moloch.

"It's the water war," he said at last, and, although his voice was harsh, there was a deep, underlying tremor in it, as if a more savage judgment had been suppressed.

"Now, Father . . . ," Gail Dundee began.

"It is, I say!"

"Seems like," said Missouri sympathetically, "there's always trouble when there isn't enough water to go around."

"There's plenty water," Dundee contradicted him. "Plenty and well divided. You're new in the

Tonopah, ain't you? Well, I'll tell you what it is. There's a meddling old crook wants to make a granger country out of the Tonopah, and he's won over some men that would have been good cattlemen, but for him!"

"A farming country, Mister Dundee?" Missouri marveled, thinking of those miles upon miles of cactus-studded dust over which they had come.

"That's it . . . they want a softy, people-crowded farming country out at the north end of the Tonopah. They want to dam the Black Gulch, and bring a hundred miles of mountain water down into the valley."

"And it wouldn't work, Mister Dundee?"

"And what if it would?" Dundee flamed. "I'm a cowman, born and bred, and hope to die a cowman. All over the West the old open-range ranches have been crowded off the map by plow and fence. The Tonopah is one of the few old-time open ranges that's left. I say . . . and I'll say it till I die . . . the men that opened this country got a right to run cattle in it if they want."

Missouri had seen old cattlemen of that mind before, and he could understand their viewpoint. The old range methods perhaps wore out their bodies as if with the dry rack, harassed them with perpetual bankruptcy, and as often as not shriveled hard-won fortunes in a single bad year. Perhaps their lives were sometimes as bleak and monotonous as the face of the desert itself. Yet

Sloper understood their love of the old long-riding ways, and their feeling of smothering entrapment as the fences closed in. He hated a fence himself.

"Horntoad Holt is back of this," Dundee went on. "I'd say it to his face the same as I say it here. I got no proof he was behind the killing of Walt Rathbone, but I say plain that no one else *could* have been back of it. And . . . it fits his ways."

"Dad, nothing but trouble can come of talking like . . ."

"Trouble?" said Dundee. "What have we ever had but trouble? I've got so I like it. Holt's coming for it, and he'll get it, and he'll get it plenty. You know Holt?" he suddenly demanded of Sloper.

"He was pointed out," Missouri said, "in Moloch. Who is this Holt?" The intense, suppressed passion of Dundee worried Sloper. Dundee was speaking injudicious—even perilous words. In all his experience, Sloper had never heard such open war talk from the mouth of a sober Westerner. It made him uneasy, and something more.

"He come here twenty years ago, stole enough cattle for a ranch, an' lived through it . . . principally due to being fast on the hammer with both hands . . . especially his right. I bet if he'd put a notch in his guns for every *hombre* he's shot it out with, them guns would look corrugated. We finally got him pinched down to where all he could lift was an occasional dogie calf. He set up to be a respectable cowman, after that, already having rustled enough to last him. Then he comes up with this infernal water project."

"If they'd just limit the water idea to improving the range for cows . . . ," Missouri started to suggest.

Dundee leveled the stem of his pipe at Missouri as if he meant to stab him with it. "That's just the infernal run-around palaver he's used. Still, the whole thing would have fallen down of its own weight, if it hadn't been for that Los Muertos copper. By heaven, I wish that copper had never been found. There was no way of raising money to build the Black Gulch dam. The government wouldn't consider it . . . not enough people affected by it. Then, pretty near a year ago, there come an unlucky day . . . Friday the Thirteenth, it must have been . . . when old Horntoad Holt and me was riding the range together, on stock count. We built a fire, and a side of rock split off under the heat . . . and there lay the Los Muertos copper, open to our eyes. Of course, it's only since that we've found out how much of that copper there is. We agreed, then, to let Walt Rathbone in on it . . . it being more his range, right there, than any one else's. And . . . I guess, somehow, we both saw even in that first hour that Holt and me was going to tangle in some way over that lode.

"We let Rathbone in, and we staked three claims in common, and called it the Three Brand Mine. Then Holt came out with his plan. He aimed to develop that lode, but none of us was to take a penny of it. Every cent from the lode was going to be put into building the Black Gulch dam. Crazy . . . you see? I bucked, bucked hard and solid. Walt Rathbone, he wavered. Morton Six, of the Moloch smelter, he surveyed the lode and offered us a mighty big price . . . more money than I thought there was in the world. I said sell. Holt said no, never. And there we've hung, in a deadlock, while the lode has laid idle all this time, and neither one of us could go ahead his way, until Walt made up his mind.

"Then, two days ago, Walt Rathbone made up his mind to sell. It meant a lot to us here, you can imagine. It's gone pretty hard with cattlemen, these last few years. And there was Gail, here, for me to think of. But we were as good as rich, the minute Walt Rathbone agreed with me to override Holt, and sell. And now . . ."

Andry Dundee was silent for a long minute. Then slowly he stood up, his body as tense as if a demon had come into him from without, and his hands raised like taut claws toward the peeled roof logs.

"Before the Almighty, no man in the world but one had reason to kill Walt Rathbone last night! I accuse Horntoad Holt!"

Gail cried out: "Dad!"

And from the doorway on Dundee's right a slow, heavy voice said: "Yeah?"

Looming darkly in the little light of the door stood the huge frame of Gideon Holt. They had not heard him come up. The approach of his horse could have been the arrival of the foreman, Lou Stam, or the stir of horses in the corral. But now that he had appeared among them, the strained silence was heavy with the imminence of sudden death.

Then Dundee's pistol whipped out. It was curious, Missouri thought afterward, that Dundee should have been wearing that gun, even while eating supper in his own house, but there it was in his hand, a black triggerless weapon with the hammer cramped back under Dundee's thumb.

Gail Dundee cried—"Dad, no!"—and flung herself upon her father. She had seized the old man's wrist, and, although he wrenched it free, he let the muzzle of the gun swing upward while, with his left arm, he swept the girl aside. Then he wavered, for Holt was leaning against the door-jamb with folded arms.

"Well, will you draw?" Dundee rasped at him.

"Can't," drawled Holt. "Left my gun belt on my saddle."

Dundee bit off an oath in his teeth, and slammed his own weapon back into the holster at his thigh.

"So you accuse me of killing Walt," said Holt. A small smile was twisting his lips, but his face was ugly.

"You heard me, I reckon," Dundee answered, his voice calmer.

"I came to ask you a question," said Holt. "Where was you last night?"

"And why should I answer that?" countered Dundee.

"Your horse has come back in," said Holt. "I passed him just now, at the spring."

"Horse back in?"

"I guess it's your horse. A Bar Five pony, ridden out, ridden out bad, with dry foam all over him, and his nose down, like no man rides out a horse, just working stock."

"What color horse?" asked Gail sharply.

"Black . . . black with a white blaze."

"That's Quartzite . . . he hasn't been ridden this week," Gail snapped at him. "Not by anybody in this outfit. That horse has been on the range, and I can name every horse ridden from here yesterday and today. Now take your insinuations out of here, and don't bring 'em back."

"Uhn-huh," said Holt softly. "I'm going now, Miss Dundee. I reckon I've found out what I come to learn. The picture ain't quite complete," he said to Dundee, his voice turning hard as granite again. "There's two or three other things I need to know. I'll find them out, all right. And when I do . . . I'll be back."

"Come shooting, then!" Dundee snarled at him.

"That's what I mean." Holt turned and removed

71

himself from the door. In the silence they heard the crunch of his boot heels and, in a moment or two, the receding hoof beats of his horse.

Dundee turned on Sloper and Law, his eyes smoking. They had not moved, and, although Holt had, for a fraction of an instant, looked Sloper squarely in the eye, he had given no sign of recognition. For a moment Dundee let his eyes bore into Missouri, then Elmer Law, then Missouri again. After that he seemed to put them out of his mind.

"You, Ricky!"

An Indian boy of fourteen or fifteen came stumbling in from the kitchen, his mouth full, but with scared eyes.

"You ride to the top of Blackcap," Dundee ordered him, "and make a fire signal to Pete and Rod on the east prairies. Signal 'em in! Don't stop to saddle. Go on, now . . . and you flog!" The boy went out, and in a minute or two they heard the diminishing beat of running hoofs, fading eastward.

"Lou Stam and Al Closson," Dundee said, half to himself and half to Gail, "are due back tonight." He sat down.

"It's a funny thing," Missouri Sloper put in tentatively, "but Morton Six said . . ."

Dundee's eyes narrowed. "You talked to Mort Six last night?"

"Yes. Elmer Law, here, was there."

"Gideon Holt in Moloch last night?" Dundee demanded sharply.

"Yes, he was." In a few words Missouri explained how he and Elmer, having heard shots and immediately stumbling over Walt Rathbone, had carried Walt into the Gun Rack Bar, how the mob action in the Gun Rack had started, and been put down by Holt, and how he and Elmer had accompanied Holt to the office of Mort Six. He omitted the hiring of himself and Elmer by Holt, although he mentioned that Holt had recognized him as a man he had known of before.

"Oh, so," commented Dundee softly. "Well, go on. What did Mort Six say?"

"He said that Rathbone had refused his final offer, once and for all. He said Rathbone's last words were . . . 'Come on with Tonopah water!'"

"His last words before he died?"

"His last words before he left the smelter office. By Six's account, Rathbone left the smelter office just about an hour before he was killed."

Dundee's face was darkening. "And where was he between?"

"I don't know."

A queer gray cast of puzzlement—or something else—had come over Dundee's features. "You sure," he bored down on Missouri, "you sure you got that right, about Rathbone refusing to sell?"

"Absolutely certain."

Dundee slowly met the startled eyes of his

daughter and held them in a long, unreadable exchange. Slowly, stiffly the old man rose. "It's half past six," he excused himself. "I've got to see about some things."

"Exactly half past?" Elmer Law asked unexpectedly.

"Six twenty-eight and a half, to be exact," said Dundee dryly.

"Well, I set my watch in Moloch," said Elmer, "and I'll bet money that you're just six and three-quarter minutes slow."

"I wouldn't doubt it," said Dundee without interest. "I forget to wind it and have to keep setting it by whatever timepiece is handy." Unsteadily he went out.

No glance passed between Missouri Sloper and Elmer Law, but a new electric charge somehow came into the air of that big rude room.

Suddenly Gail Dundee reached across the corner of the table to grasp Missouri's wrist. A quick thrill shot through him at the touch of the girl's hand, but he found her eyes cool, steady, and direct.

"What are you doing here?"

"Miss Dundee, I'm a cowman looking for a job."

"And that's all? You swear that?"

"Yes . . . of course. What did you think?"

"Then," said the girl, "that's all right. Just forget it. But if you're anything else . . . cowboy, ride."

"What else would I be?"

"Nothing. Just forget it."

But he already knew he was going to forget nothing this girl ever said.

IV

Lou Stam and Al Closson rode in at dusk. They came in five minutes apart, Closson first, on a wet and punished-looking horse. This was a small wiry man with a sand-carved face and a hard eye. Lou Stam came in more leisurely. In contrast to Closson, Stam's speech was a soft drawl, and everything about the man was easy, relaxed, and slow. He had half-mournful, half-reticent blue eyes, and a quiet, poker player's face—until he smiled. Lou Stam's smile was his best bet, for it was humorous, ingratiating, and infectious.

"Best range boss in the Tonopah," Dundee introduced him, and Stam saluted gravely, without, however, offering to shake hands.

After that, Law and Missouri Sloper were shown bunks in the bunkhouse, which was a long one-room adobe, a little apart from the main house. Al Closson and Elmer Law turned in at once, and were soon snoring. Lou Stam, however, after half an hour's smoking beside the door of the bunkhouse, got out a banjo and wandered off to a retreat behind the corral, from which point he presently stirred the night with mournful song.

Missouri turned in, but for a long time lay awake, with no sleep in his thoughts. Presently he gave up the attempt, pulled on his clothes, and went for a walk in the outer air. Given no particular place to go, a cowboy always heads either for the kitchen or the corral—the two principal factors in the natural course of his existence, and it was to the latter that Sloper unconsciously wandered now.

A lonely figure sat on the corral's top rail, silhouetted against the starry desert sky. Even at first glance, Missouri somehow knew who this was. " 'Evenin' Miss Dundee."

"Howdy, boy."

"I'm right pleased to see you," said Missouri. "There was something I wanted to ask you about."

"Have a seat," Gail Dundee invited him. "But be quiet about it . . . I'm not supposed to be out here."

"You're not supposed . . . ?"

"Everybody around here is so jumpy lately," Gail explained. "Dad especially. You can hardly make a move without stirring up all kinds of foolish racket about it. I don't know what's got into the Tonopah."

"Well, of course," said Missouri, swinging up to a seat beside her on the fence, "this water war . . ."

"I suppose that's at the bottom of it. But . . . still, sometimes it seems . . . oh, I don't know. It isn't as nice 'round here as it used to be. I know that. Poor Jimmy!"

"Who's Jimmy?"

"Jimmy Rathbone. A nice boy, you can't help liking him. But he'll never be able to hold the Crazy K together, never in the world."

"He inherits a third interest in the Los Muertos copper, too?"

"Yes, I expect so."

"And do you suppose he'll swing with your father, or with Holt?"

"You mean for the quick money or for the water? Oh, he'll sell out cold, I suppose." Missouri Sloper carefully weighed the tone of her voice. For an instant he thought he had detected in it a trace of contempt. "I'm sure I don't know," she added coolly.

They were talking in whispers. Slowly and distinctly through the night drifted the words of Lou Stam's song, from somewhere off in the dark, 100 yards away.

> Tony, why-y you come to Montan'?
> Why you gamble with Winnipeg Dan?
> Why you pull-a da knife?
> Why you lose-a da life?
> Oh, why you come to Montan'?

"He's got a right pretty voice," Sloper admitted.

"Lou is a right pretty man," said Gail softly.

"Like him pretty well, don't you?"

"What was it you wanted to ask me about?"

"I've been wondering what you meant," said Missouri, "when you asked me if I was really just a rider looking for a job?"

The directness of the girl's reply amazed him. "I thought maybe you were a gunfighter."

"Gunfight . . . say, do I look like . . . ?"

"Do gunfighters look any particular way?"

"No, I guess not," Missouri admitted. "Well, I realized that I was a real homely character."

"It isn't that. I don't think you're any homelier than lots of people. Kind of nice, rather."

"Oh, sure," agreed Missouri. "But why a gunfighter? Are you having an inflow of desperate characters?"

"No, not exactly. Of course, there have been rumors. Maybe you noticed what Dad said about trouble smoking up."

They were silent, and to them came the clear lazy words of Lou Stam's lonely serenade.

> Tony, why you rush-a da can?
> Why you cuss-a da gambolin' man?
> Why you fight-a like hell?
> Don' you know pretty well
> That's just plain suicide in Montan'?

"Never heard that song," commented Missouri. "Funny one, all right."

"I don't think it's funny. I think it's kind of sad."

"Sad? The way it's sung, you mean?"

She ignored this. "It's just about some little misfit foreigner that headed into something that was too much for him. Anybody's liable to do that, cowboy."

"I see what you mean," said Missouri.

"Only," Gail Dundee went on, "the song makes out somebody cared about him and was sorry. But here's what . . . the fellow that's singing it, he figures nobody would care about the same thing if it happened to *him* . . . and that's what he's really singing about. But at the same time, he's trying to laugh at himself. See?"

"I never thought about it just that way."

"Of course," she said, still in those soft, husky whispers, "he wouldn't cry about it himself . . . he sings lightly enough. But listen to that banjo . . . hear it cry? Just like its heart would break."

"He has that banjo whipped all right. But . . . you mean he's thinking how sad it would be if he got killed or something?"

"No, that isn't it."

"I don't get it then."

She was silent, and another stanza came swaggering across the dark, but this time, underneath the words, Missouri got the sob of the banjo, thrumming its heart out in some obscure grief.

Tony, why you forget da bambin'?
Why you not stay in Saline?

79

Maria, she weep . . .
You don' care, you so deep
Down under da State of Montan'.

"Don't you?" Her shoulder was close to his, as they sat there six feet off the ground on the top rail of the corral. She turned her head to look him fully in the face. Her face, so near his own, was very beautiful, he thought, in the light of the stars.

"Well," said Gail almost inaudibly, "Lou's singing that song to me."

It was as if his horse had suddenly slipped on a steep trail and gone from under him. So that was why she was sitting out here alone? Listening to a song that was sung for her—although the singer perhaps didn't know exactly where she was, or if she was listening. Yes, that banjo was eloquent, all right—too eloquent.

"I guess," said Missouri slowly, "I guess maybe I don't belong sitting here. I guess maybe I'm just sitting into a game that was all stacked against me, before ever I showed over the hill."

"What do you mean?"

"If it's set up for him to sing and you to listen . . ."

"If it was stacked that way, would the banjo be crying so?"

"I'll say this for Lou Stam," said Missouri, "though I've seen him only once. He knows how to sit a horse."

"Doesn't he, though? Did you notice the shape

his horse was in as he rode up? He'd been gone since yesterday morning, and that was the same horse he started out with. Yet that pony was just as fresh as if he'd only that minute been roped."

"Yes, I saw. He sure can ride, all right."

Here the banjo thrumming dwindled to a low pumping and came nearer. Gail Dundee slid to the ground.

"I don't know what there is about you makes me talk so much," she told him. "Good night." She lost herself, light-footed, in the shadows of the pepper trees.

Back in the bunkhouse, Al Closson was still snoring. Missouri sat down on the edge of his bunk and covered his face with his hands. Elmer Law, always a fits-and-starts sleeper, sat up and struck fire for a cigarette. Suddenly Elmer let his cigarette go unlighted to hold the flame of the match in Missouri's face.

"You sick?" Law demanded

"No, I'm not sick."

"See a ghost?"

"No."

"Nor a murder?"

"No."

"What is gone to hell? You look fit to hit."

"This," said Missouri, "is just about the saddest row I ever sat in at, Elmer."

Elmer Law sighed gustily. "It sure is."

"What the hell do *you* know about it?"

"I've always been one of the most popular men in the West," said Elmer Law inaccurately, "until I come here. I've never seen us so swift and sudden disliked. Al Closson don't like us because he don't like anybody. Old Dundee don't like us because we belong to the human race. Gail don't like us because she strings along with her paw. The Chinese cook don't like us because we make dirty dishes. And Lou Stam's got it in for us because you gone sweet on Gail. I'm going to get out of this . . ."

"What was that last?" Missouri cut him off.

"I said, a blind man could see with his cane that you've gone sweet on Dundee's daughter."

"I wouldn't talk so much, Elmer, if I was you."

"When two honest cowboys can't ride up to a *rancho* without being took for gunmen, it's time to leave the range."

"We're not leaving, Elmer. You, maybe . . . but not we."

"Maybe," said Elmer slowly, "I've noticed a couple of things you didn't. There's considerable under the surface around here, what with murders in the smoke and unanimous declarations of hell and general war. Here's what gives me the creeps. If I was offered thirty-seven dollars to walk out tonight, and call the turn on that murder . . . I could do it. But I wouldn't . . . not for a million."

"Nor me, Elmer," said Missouri softly.

They looked at each other through the dark. "You got a hunch, too?" said Elmer Law.

"I wish to heaven," said Missouri, "I could answer no."

"Least said, soonest escaped with our lives," said Elmer, and he turned his face to the wall.

Breakfast at the Dundee ranch was eaten in a brittle silence. Gail Dundee did not appear.

"Mister Dundee," said Missouri Sloper when he had saddled his horse, "we sure thank you for the oats."

"That's all right," said Dundee glumly.

"I guess we'll be staggering on now, unless . . ."

"Unless what?"

Missouri did not hesitate. "We're looking for work, Mister Dundee, and we thought that, if you was able to use a couple of able-bodied cowpokes, there's hardly anybody we'd rather do out of a couple months' pay than yourself."

"I got nothing for you," said Andry Dundee shortly. "You're not likely to find jobs in the Tonopah, I'll tell you that."

"Might that be a personal remark, Mister Dundee?" said Missouri after a little pause.

"No, nothing like that," Dundee amended. "There's too many people in the Tonopah for what the range will support . . . that's all. I don't know where all the people come from, wanting riding jobs and all. Well, all I got to say is, this darned wave of population will just have to pass on over and go by. It ain't wanted here."

"Good many riding through?"

"I suppose there's been at least half a dozen in the last ten months alone."

"That's a heap of fellers, all right," said Missouri without expression.

"More than enough," Dundee grumbled.

"We'd like to stay in the Tonopah, if we could. We'll have a look around."

Dundee studied Missouri narrowly. "Horntoad Holt send you here?" he asked unexpectedly.

"In a way, Mister Dundee," said Missouri without apology.

"In a way?" Dundee's face was darkening, and the brassy glow was returning to his deep-set eyes.

"We don't know Holt much," Missouri explained. "We struck him for a job in Moloch. He said come and talk it over with you. I got the idea that, if we got no jobs here, Holt would try to fix us up."

"Gunfighter?" demanded Dundee, his voice suddenly sharp as the cut of a quirk.

"That's three times I've been asked that in the Tonopah. I don't like that hint very well, Mister Dundee. I don't feel called on to answer it, either, but I will. I give it the flat lie."

There was a long moment of silence, while Dundee glared into the quiet steady eyes of Sloper.

"I give you one warning," said Dundee finally. "It's my first and my last. By steady riding you can be out of the Tonopah tonight. Don't let sunrise throw your shadow in the Tonopah tomorrow."

"Or else?" inquired Sloper.

"You had your warning. Now get off my place and off my range, and, if ever again you meet me in the Tonopah, draw and fire, for I'll pistol-whip you just as sure as my name's Dundee."

For a moment Sloper sat silently, then he saluted gravely, and wheeled his horse.

"Just stay around, Mister Sloper," Elmer Law advised when they were out of earshot. "Just stay right around . . . and take your choice between getting shot, or killing the girl's pa."

"It's a pretty one, all right," Missouri admitted.

V

The Holt bunkhouse was adobe like Dundee's, and there was a long adobe stable and three pole corrals. But the house in which Gideon Holt himself kept bachelor hall was a mud shack of one room, with a skimpy gallery of warped boards tacked on in front, and a roof of dry-rotted and shackling staves—the hole-up of a man whose personal comfort never entered his head.

Old Horntoad Holt was standing in his door, waiting for Sloper and Law, as they came up. He was wearing ancient chaps and brush jacket, and a .30-30 Winchester rested in the crook of his arm. Somehow he looked a good deal like a bear brought to stand. Certainly the angry assurance had gone out of him, giving place to a curious puzzled, frustrated air—the look of a man surrounded by enemies invisible and unknown. His two heavy guns swung holstered at his thighs, and he was as much a fighting man as ever, only, Sloper would have said, Holt no longer knew who he was fighting.

"Well?" said Holt.

"We did what you said," Sloper told him.

Holt was studying Missouri Sloper. "I see the balance has shifted," he said after a moment or two. He allowed himself a faint smile. "Night before last, in Moloch, you suspected Mort Six, and I suspected Dundee. Now that you've been to Dundee and spoke your piece . . . you suspect Dundee yourself."

Elmer Law shifted uncomfortably.

"I didn't say that," said Missouri without expression. "I don't say it now."

"You don't need to," said Holt, his eyes steadily upon Missouri's face. "Yep, you suspect Dundee, and for some reason you're sure sorry. Oh . . . on account of Gail Dundee. Well, I don't blame you for being struck with Gail Dundee."

The man on the horse and the man on the ground confronted each other in a curiously long stare.

There was a faint ironic gleam in the eye of Horntoad Holt, and, although Missouri's face remained expressionless, Elmer Law chuckled as he saw that here, for once, Missouri did not have the upper hand.

"Mind reading?" said Missouri at last.

"Guessing," said Holt. "Well . . . you still want to work for the Cross Hook brand, now that you've heard what Andry Dundee aims to do to it?"

"This morning," said Missouri Sloper, "Dundee asked me if I had come there from you. And when he'd heard the facts, he promised to shoot on sight if he met me in the Tonopah again."

"Figured I'd called in a ringer to gunfight for me," Holt grunted. "And now . . ."

But I tell you this," Sloper said. "I'll never raise gun to Andry Dundee, nor take any part in any conviction of him, nor work against him in any way."

"On account of the girl being his daughter, you mean?"

"My cards are on the table. You can read them to suit you, or as they lie. But I'm not leaving the Tonopah, Mister Holt . . . not while this here fight goes on."

"You begin to sound like a feller I could use in my employ," said Holt. "I was pretty sure that any fellers who lasted four years with Bob MacIntyre would fit into the Cross Hook."

"After what I've just said . . . and you fighting Dundee?"

"I'm fighting the killer of Walt Rathbone . . . for the present," Holt corrected. "And right now I don't see how it could be Dundee, or anybody backed by him. Come here a minute."

He led the way to one of the three pole corrals, beyond the shanty. Half a dozen horses stood about in the trampled dust, but Sloper instantly noticed one of them in particular—a sweaty and foam-streaked bay pony that stood loosely under saddle. The reins of the bridle were gone, and the bit dangled loosely at one side of the broken headstall as if the reins had been trampled and torn off. The saddle was canted, as if the horse had rolled, trying to free himself of it. And the canted saddle was streaked with dark stains.

"Harry Stucky rode that horse over to the Three Brand Mine yesterday . . . nineteen miles northwest. That horse came in an hour ago. Art Humphreys has taken the back trail of the critter . . . I've only kept three riders this year, and Art's all that's left here. I'm riding straight to Los Muertos Vivientes, the hills that the Three Brand discovery is in. If you hone to sit into this mess, I won't refuse you, but I tell you plain, I don't know what's happening, nor what I'm riding into. There may be a fight in Los Muertos, but I don't know against who or how many, nor why. My hunch is that the same thing is behind the murder of Rathbone and the murder of Stucky . . . if he's dead. If you look forward to a long life . . . good bye. Personally I advise you to pull out."

"Elmer and me will need fresh horses," Sloper said, "if we're going to clip off that nineteen miles to Los Muertos hills."

Holt stuck out his hand, and they shook. "I see you caught old MacIntyre's everlasting thirst for trouble," was all he said.

"You can call it that," said Sloper slowly. He was thinking, though, of something else.

Elmer Law heaved a long sigh.

"There's cornbread and cold fried bacon in the cook shack, but don't be long," Holt said. "For horses, take anything in that other corral. And I've got rifles for you here."

For three hours they rode northwestward over a desert studded with the scattered, grotesquely bristling shapes of Joshua trees, between which occasional small bands of scrub cattle wandered, seeking the short wisps of sand grass. Then they topped a long lava-broken rise, and Holt drew in his horse.

"Los Muertos Vivientes," he said, "the Mountains of the Living Dead."

From the rim of the world a spur of the Warbonnets rose, striking southeasterly, so that the westering sun turned their tipper peaks to a fairyland glory of red gold, modeled in the pale blue of distance and chased with the silver of everlasting snows. But between the riders and the tall Warbonnets loomed a nearer range, black and hideous, blotting out all but the high rim of the tall sun-magic mountains beyond.

The range called Los Muertos Vivientes struck southwesterly, so that the aspect they approached was untouched by the sun, and the vast folds and crags of Los Muertos struck upon the spirit of Missouri Sloper heavily with the impact of a new prophetic dread. That dark twisted range was like sad, terrible music, or the lost hope of a world. One peak only caught a red touch of the sunset, as if it were wet with blood. The man who named those hills must have seen them thus, sad and black and hopeless at sunset, when he named them the Mountains of the Living Dead.

"The Three Brand copper strike is in that fourth gulch, as you come at it from the south," said Holt. Suddenly his manner changed, and he pointed northward toward the high rim of the world. "And yonder you can just see the mouth of Black Gulch, the key to five thousand miles of watershed and the Tonopah water. You know where all that water goes? Into these sands under us. Down under these dry sands is the water, under the Tonopah. Irrigation would draw that water up . . . they call it bringing up the sub. And here, a few feet above . . . gaunted cattle, dying on the sand."

Suddenly Holt reached out and gripped Sloper's elbow, the light of a fanatic in his eyes. "Can't you see it? Running water . . . alfalfa . . . stirrup-high grass, ranch houses in groves of trees, a big breed of cattle, and plenty money, and garden truck on the tables, and young folks swarming at the barn dances after roundup . . ." The glow faded out of his eyes. "But Dundee wants a desert . . . a thousand miles of lonesome sand, fit only to keep a little handful of people shanty poor. And he's going to have it, it seems. After"—he added—"after me, the old Horntoad, is dead."

The vast black despair that was Los Muertos had thrown a sense of prophecy into Missouri Sloper, and he was wondering if old Horntoad Holt was going to meet the death of which he spoke in that dismal range—perhaps someday, perhaps tonight.

"It sure looks sordid," said Elmer.

Although every detail of that black range was clear through the lucid desert air, another hour elapsed while they approached, and dusk was closing fast, when at last they neared the gulch of the Three Brand Mine.

Suddenly, without warning of any kind, Elmer Law's horse grunted as if kicked in the stomach, and pitched on buckling knees nose first into the sand. An instant later the sound of a shot came to them from high in the uptilted rock through which cut the Three Brand Gulch. It echoed and reëchoed, and before the echoes died they were wakened again, and again, as sand spurted beyond the riders, and to either hand.

Sloper whirled his horse, striking the spurs hard. Elmer Law was getting up from the saddle of his dying pony. Sloper offered him an arm as he galloped past, and Law swung up behind him. At 200 yards only ricochets were droning about them. At 300 the sound of these had died away, and the firing from the hills had ceased, as the riders drew out of range.

"Lucky shot," grunted Holt. "Gets a horse the first crack . . . and at the very outside limit of rifle reach!"

"If he'd only waited," said Sloper, "he could have got us all."

"He didn't dast wait," said Holt. "What that boy wants is us out of here. Come on. I'll bet he never makes it out. Pocketed, by gum."

Holt led off in a wide, sweeping circle, galloping hard, so that Sloper had to punish his double-laden horse in order to keep up. Up a long slope Holt pushed, well to one side of the Three Brand Gulch, and in a nest of scant manzanita Holt swung down.

"Law, take the horses. It's up to you to keep them safe . . . and see that nobody rides straight out the mouth of that gulch. Lead up that rise, quick, to pretty near the crest, then picket and crawl ahead to the top of the rise. You got maybe twelve minutes. Then you'll be looking down on the mouth of the gulch, with half a moon to shoot by, pretty quick, and a range of maybe four hundred. Git!"

Elmer Law went clattering up the rock-strewn steep, the led horses at his heels.

"Sloper, strike the gulch high, and keep going until you come to a balanced rock on the gulch rim. From there you take under fire a goat trail on the far side, at maybe six hundred yards. That miscreant fired on us from a place where horses can't go. He can't leave until he drops down into the gulch after his horse, and most likely his partner. You'll be covering one of the two likely ways."

"And you?"

"I'm foot racing 'em to the main back way out of that. I can beat 'em to the top all right, because I'm afoot. But what I want is to meet 'em as they come, and the deeper into their territory the better."

"Who is it?" Sloper called after him.

"God knows," Holt sung back. He was gone, a scrambling gaunt shadow between broken rocks.

Sloper was already on his way. He climbed for perhaps twenty minutes, while all around him the desolate rock of Los Muertos rose more bitterly sharp, more steeply. When he had climbed for a long time, he thought he must have missed his way, and was attacked by that sense of awful futility a man feels when he has let his comrades down and is mystified to know how he failed.

But he found the balanced rock at last, and climbed a ragged spur of granite on hands and knees, pushing his rifle ahead of him.

Below him, as he came to the sharp rim of the granite, empty space dropped away, the dim gray shadows of the cleft so disguising the floor of the gulch as to give the impression of an unlimited abyss. But Missouri's eyes were hunting something else, in the better light of the higher steeps. What he sought was neither path nor trail, but simply a way—any possible way—up which a mounted man could climb out of that dismal gulch. And presently his mountain-trained eyes found such a way, and he knew it for the goat trail of which Holt had spoken.

That way out for the unknown enemy was unmarked by so much as a goat track, and only the fact that its intricacy of ledge and steep was the only continuous footing for horses made it recognizable for the trail Sloper sought. At the top that lone way out ended on a broad bulge of granite, an ugly-looking bit of footing, but Sloper knew that it offered no particular hazard to a horse, even if shod. What interested him, as the night closed heavily upon the hills of Los Muertos Vivientes, was that a rider could not bulge across that high granite without silhouetting himself against the moonlit sky.

He estimated the range carefully by more than one device, and concluded it was possibly more, but certainly not less than 600 yards. Then he set himself to wait.

He had not, however, as long to wait as he had supposed. Five minutes had hardly passed when Sloper detected the muffled hoof placements of a walking horse in the gorge below. The sound seemed to indicate an animal coming downcañon from above, which was not what he had expected nor did he understand how, if their assumptions of position had been correct, the unseen rider far below had come along so soon. There must, Missouri judged, be others besides the man who had fired upon them as they rode up from the plain. He waited, wondering how many were to join the upcañon rider before the miscreants attempted to leave the gulch. That they would leave he was sure; no one in his right mind would attempt an illegal seize against the cowboy of the Three Brand.

Another five minutes passed, while the rider climbed the goat trail that Missouri watched, before man and animal became visible in the better light of the upper ledges. No others had joined the rider from upcañon. The watched man moved slowly. He was, Missouri concluded, mounted upon an unusually good mountain horse—a buckskin that walked quietly and was very sure-footed.

Missouri Sloper had already admitted to himself that he would not be able to shoot down an unarmed man, even though that man be one who had attempted to kill him from cover. His plan was to shoot over the man's head as the other reached the foot of that exposed bulge of granite, where the certainty of his marksmanship would be at its best. If the other man turned back, without exposing himself against the skyline, Holt would be left with his own killing to do, at his own discretion, as the rider attempted the rear way out of the gulch—which was Missouri's idea of things as they should be.

Slowly the rider advanced up the goat walk of the cañon wall. Twice he drew in his horse, as if listening. It was unlikely that he would stop merely to breathe his animal, Missouri thought, under the circumstances. The unknown rider had reached the base of the granite.

Missouri fired once, and by the quick jerk of the distant horse he knew that his lead had spattered the granite very close. Down his dimly visible gunsights he watched the next move of the man from the gulch.

The rider did not hesitate. Sloper saw the man's elbows come up as he bent forward in the saddle; he even sensed the shock of spurs on horseflesh, as the animal went up the granite in spraddled, laboring bounds, like a mountain lion on treacherous footing.

A running horse made a tricky mark at 600 yards, considering the bad light. Missouri drew as good a bead as he could upon the animal's fugitive quarters. At this mark he twice fired and missed. Horse and rider abruptly reached the skyline, and for the first time showed distinctly as a rifle mark. Missouri had perhaps fifteen seconds more, he estimated, before horse and rider should disappear. With elbows braced on the rock and his cheek steady against the stock, Sloper slowly drew his final line upon the escaping horseman. This time he had no intention of missing.

Then suddenly—Missouri Sloper swore to himself, and his rifle muzzle swung up as he relaxed his aim. The rider on the granite bulge had at the last minute given the horse its head, and swung about in the saddle with drawn six-shooter, evidently in the hope of sending at least one half random replying shot across the gulch. And by the wiry movement of the rider's sway in the saddle, by the glimpsed tilt of the hat—but chiefly perhaps by means of recognition which he could not have defined, but in which he rested full faith—Sloper was suddenly sure that the man upon whom he fired was Andry Dundee.

Angry and astonished, but above all puzzled, Sloper watched his man making good his escape. That Dundee had fired upon Sloper and his companions he could hardly believe, yet he knew it was not only possible but likely. He swung aside his rifle, as Dundee finally fired, the shot going nowhere.

In that instant a rifle crashed unexpectedly above Missouri and to his left, and Sloper saw Dundee—if it was Dundee—crumple and slump headlong from the saddle. For the moment Sloper hardly stopped to question the source of the shot in the swift shock of its result. Whatever that fallen man might have done, whatever manner of man he might be, he was still of the flesh and blood of Gail Dundee.

For a horrible moment Sloper thought that the struck man's foot was caught in the stirrup, and that he was to see that fallen form smashed to a pulp by the hoofs of the horse and the swift merciless drag over the broken rocks beyond the bulge of granite. The horse was rearing and shying sideways, somehow restrained from bolting. Then, with a shock of what he had to admit was relieved surprise, he saw that the fallen man was not dead, but clinging to the reins of his mount. He was struggling up; he was trying to subdue the frantic animal that reared and shied and struck as it avoided its fallen rider.

Sloper saw the downed man gain the animal's head and get a grip on the saddle horn at last— and finally regain the saddle awkwardly, as the pony bolted over the rim of the world.

Meanwhile, from the rim on Sloper's left the unknown rifle spoke repeatedly. Counting back in his memory Sloper knew that the gunner had fired four times more, as rapidly as he could pump the lead. By this time Sloper had come to the conclusion that this unheralded support could be credited to no one but Gideon Holt. Holt's marksmanship, he reflected, as he stood up and snapped fresh cartridges into the magazine of his rifle, was not what it was cracked up to be by any means. By the hurried shooting he would have expected to find that Elmer Law had come to his support, but Elmer would have obeyed orders, whereas Holt, perhaps hearing that sound of the hoofs as the lone horsemen rode downcañon toward the out trail, must have changed his purpose and . . .

To Missouri's ears came the faint, soft slip of metal on metal, and a gentle *click*. It was the sound of a cartridge pumped into its chamber, which was natural enough, but it had not been the sharp metallic snap made by the reloading of an angry and disappointed man, but the stealthy, cautious bullet chambering of someone who prepared to fire, yet wished to keep his position unknown.

Missouri flung himself face down upon the ground. He could not get down quickly enough to suit him—gravity was too slow, and every muscle of his body strained for an instant in a futile effort to pull the mountain up against himself, to flatten behind the cover of the scattered rocks. He was not a split second too soon. As Missouri dropped, the unknown rifleman fired. Sloper's eyes caught the quick angry stab of the powder blaze from a point hardly thirty yards away, and so short was the range that the smash of the report could not be separated from the vicious zip of the lead that passed over.

"Whoof!" Missouri blew out a violent breath of relief. He liked living mighty well, and annihilation had passed him so close that he imagined he had felt its clammy breath. Relief was followed by a swift flash of anger. Leaving his rifle under him, he jerked his handier Colt from its holster, wormed sharply to the right, and, from around the corner of a rock like a tombstone, smashed out a shot at a fragment of moving shadow. The shadow—its exposed portion had been no bigger than a man's hand—jerked out of sight.

The quick twilight of the southwest ranges was now utterly gone, and the promised moon, no more than a silver shaving, seemed unable to penetrate the black folds of Los Muertos. Peering out from a new place, Missouri's eyes could make out nothing of use to him. He was in a high, ragged country of split granite, of twisted scrub juniper and piñon, punctuated here and there by conical-trunked sugar pines so stunted by the altitude that a tree with a six-foot base rose but twenty or thirty feet into the air. In this broken cover an army could move unseen, and a lone bushwhacker could dodge about forever without making his whereabouts known.

The stealth with which his enemy had moved, however, and the manner in which he had attempted to down Missouri from cover at almost point-blank range gave the rimrock veteran a pretty dependable knowledge of what the man would try next. In all probability the ambusher would creep away at the first opportunity; conceivably he had already done so. "Attack like a lion, run like a sheep," was a mountain proverb that applied to others besides the now tamed Apaches. A man who shot from cover could be depended upon to avoid the hazard of a creeping gunfight among the rocks.

Missouri Sloper sat up behind the rock that sheltered him, turned his back to it and his enemy, and leaned against the stone to roll a cigarette. He could not, of course, strike a light as yet, but he had plenty of time now to wait the other out, make a careful cigarette, and think.

Ten minutes passed, fifteen. Sloper heard a small grating sound of pressure upon gravel—so small that it could hardly have been a boot heel, yet might have been a man resting weight on the heel of his hand, as he crept. Missouri could not tell the exact distance, but was sure that the sound came from much more than the original thirty yards away. He smiled dryly. In a crawling fight in the dark an attacker had no chance; the man who waited out the other invariably won if he kept his head. If his unknown enemy was not going to attack, the matter was closed, as far as Missouri was concerned.

Much later Missouri Sloper heard the receding hoof beats of a horse put abruptly into a run from a point some distance away.

Judging his skirmish in the rocks to be over with, but cautious yet, Missouri shifted his position to a place where the rock formations would mask the glow of his cigarette, and lit up, muffling the flare of the match in his hands.

Before the cigarette was finished, a new stealthy approach caused him to snuff out the red coal. A man either in moccasins or his sock feet was coming carefully toward him from below, and, by the occasional small sounds that gave the newcomer away, Missouri Sloper judged that the man would pass him very closely. He silently took yet a new position, this time one that, through a jagged slit between two sharp-broken blocks of granite, overlooked the way the fellow would come.

Now a figure, dim in the faintly translucent darkness, appeared, half crouching, from cover sixty yards away. It was the figure of a man who carried his rifle at the ready and his boots under one arm. Gently Sloper got his rifle up and sighted it approximately upon the third button of the stalker's shirt. Then disgustedly he let his rifle down again. The man who so cautiously approached was Elmer Law.

Sloper waited until his partner had approached

within six feet of his position and was about to pass by before he spoke. Then: "Looking for someone, bud?"

Elmer Law jumped, whirled, and dropped a boot.

"Oh, hello, Missouri!"

"Hello, hell! Do you realize you pretty near killed me a few minutes ago?"

"Who? Me? How?"

"By shooting at me, damn it!"

"It couldn't have been me, Missouri. I haven't had a chance at a shot, not even at you, let alone anybody that amounted to anything."

"*Hmm*. That's different, then," Sloper admitted. "In that case . . . maybe you'd better get your head down, Elmer."

Elmer Law eased himself to a squat, his eyes searching the ragged rims of Los Muertos.

"I heard you shooting, but you haven't begun bragging, so I suppose you missed. You sure threw enough lead around, to judge by the racket."

"I was only one of the parties," Sloper told him. In a few words he described to Elmer Law what had happened. Elmer said he had heard the horse that had just left the vicinity at a run, but had not seen it or its rider. After what had seemed to Law a long time without action, he had given up the watching at the cañon mouth, and had come up to join the battle in which Missouri seemed to be embroiled.

Grimly the partners looked at each other through the semidarkness.

"And you didn't recognize who it was that got gunned off his horse across the cañon?"

Missouri did not reply at once. "I'm not certain," he said at last, "that I did."

"But you got a pretty good idea," Elmer interpreted. "I guess I see your meaning, all right, Missouri. I'll keep shut my mouth until you're ready to speak. It's hell, all right."

"It sure is," said Missouri.

"I think we ought to move on out of this Tonopah country," Elmer said. "You see where signs are pointing? Looks like to me Dundee has overplayed his hand. He's going to get closed in on just as sure as hell gets sheepmen. And the way we're fixed here, we're coming pretty near to helping close in. Not so good, when you stop to think that, after all, his daughter is a mighty pretty girl. It isn't her fault if her pa's turned killer, but it isn't our fault, either, and I say let's get out of this business."

Sloper considered. "Not yet," he said finally.

"This thing'll trail out forever," moaned Elmer.

"It'll be over within three days."

"There's some ain't going to live to see the end of it at all, Missouri," Elmer contended.

"I'm afraid that's so."

"And what about us?"

"I'm playing a long chance, Elmer . . . the

chance that Dundee is innocent. He's in a bad fix . . . a whole lot worse than maybe you know, certainly worse than he knows. But I mean to do what I can to get him out . . . if it can be done."

"And then . . . ?"

"Good bye, Tonopah."

"And all this on account of Gail Dundee?"

"Is that your business?"

"More like my finish," Elmer mourned.

Slowly Missouri looked over this man who seemed to have no purpose in life but to stand by his friend, and he relented.

"Well . . . you're pretty near right, Elmer, I guess."

"It is Gail, then?"

Missouri nodded. "Three days more."

VI

What Missouri Sloper and Elmer Law would have liked to do would have been to get in touch with Gideon Holt, but with Holt on the stalk this was impossible. The intricacies of Three Brand Gulch were unknown to either Missouri or Elmer Law, nor did they know who else might be waiting to take another shot from ambush at the next easy mark. In the end they returned to the horses and set themselves to wait. Hours passed.

"It makes my scalp crawl," Elmer confided.

"Who killed who? What for? We haven't even got a good idea of what the war is about. I thought I did. I thought it was a simple row over whether the Three Brand Mine was to be exploited for the benefit of water, or otherwise. But here's hell broke out in a new place. What's the meaning?"

"I'll tell you pretty soon," Missouri encouraged him.

"I know this . . . this is an unsafe country. I'd as lief be back in Indian days as . . . Up your hands, you by them ponies, or I'll blast . . . !"

"Save your powder," came Holt's weary voice.

"You sure made a nice quiet approach," Sloper complimented him.

"Didn't know who I'd find here. Get anybody? I heard firing at this end."

"We jumped four, five fellers, but they got loose from us," said Elmer.

"Four, five?"

"Well . . . two, anyway."

Missouri Sloper retailed his account of the man who had left the gulch by the trail on the other side, and of the other unknown who had fired on that man, then turned to try to gun down Sloper himself from cover. He did not, however, mention the name of Dundee.

Horntoad Holt nodded morosely. "I found Harry Stucky," he told them.

"Dead?" said Sloper.

Holt nodded. "Seemed like he was shot from

above as he rode up the gulch, but he managed to get his horse turned and rode about fifty yards before he fell. Then he dragged himself behind a boulder, facing upcañon, and there he died, his gun in his hand, without firing a shot. A good man, too. . . ."

"We better eat something," suggested Elmer.

"Yeah. I got to be getting back after that. I got to kill a man. This clears Dundee. There's another dead man in that gulch that we ain't found yet."

"How do you know that?"

"The law has it that you have to do one hundred dollars' assessment work on every unpatented mining claim every year, or your rights lapse. The year on the Three Brand runs out the latter part of this week. But with modern equipment, such as mules and dynamite, it doesn't take very much time to run up to the requirement in yardage moved. So two weeks ago I sent an outfit of Mexicans and equipment under Rod Laughlin up here to hustle through the assessment work. Well . . . the assessment work isn't done."

"Not done?"

"Not a shovel full of earth turned."

"And the Mexicans . . . ?"

"Cleared out. Rod Laughlin, I couldn't find any sign of. This I know. Rod would have done his best and shot square. I can't believe he's living today. I couldn't tell what happened, it was so dark in that fold. There's a dead mule up there, though."

"Does this mean you lose the mine?"

"Well, no, not necessarily." Horntoad Holt got up suddenly. "I'm thinking more about Rod and Walt and Harry than about the damn' mine . . . though I figured it meant the Tonopah water once. Sloper, do this for me . . . we're shy a horse anyway. Stay here and see what you can trace out in the sign up at the Three Brand Mine. You'll find it all right . . . there's been a wagon gone up, when we sent in the outfit. See if you can find Rod Laughlin, and whatever else you can. And pile a few rocks over poor Harry Stucky. I'll send Elmer back with a horse for you. Me, I'll be back when I've killed Mort Six."

"You think Mort Six . . . ?"

"Who else," Holt flamed, "is interested in seeing our title lapse on this mine? Who's wanted this lode all along, and who couldn't get it at any price? Mort Six! Well, I'll give him an even break on the draw . . . and see you in a couple of days if I'm alive and a free man." He scratched a note on a page of his tally book, and handed it to Sloper. "If Art Humphreys gets here . . . you'll know him by his pinto . . . show him this. It'll tell him who you are."

When Holt and Elmer Law had ridden southward on the two remaining horses, Missouri Sloper sat for a long time, smoking a cigarette the coal of which he was careful not to expose. Mort Six, although Sloper had seen him but once, decidedly did not fit into the picture of the crimes that stood unsolved in the Tonopah—the killing of Walt Rathbone and Harry Stucky, and possibly of Rod Laughlin, and the attempt by the concealed rifleman in the cañon. To jump a claim by gun-shot was simply not the sort of project that Mort Six would be expected to conceive. Further exculpating Mort Six was the curious, vague involvement of Dundee, who Sloper believed to have been in Moloch the night of Rathbone's murder, yet who was concealing this and who had certainly tonight been in the Three Brand Gulch where one, and possibly two men lay dead.

And yet, what could be Dundee's possible motive for wishing to have the triple claim on the Three Brand lapse? And who was the man who had fired across the gulch at Dundee, and later tried to kill Sloper? Missouri wished fervently that Dundee had not promised to shoot him on sight—he would have liked to ask a question or two of Dundee.

The last of the night was still draining away in purple shadows from the Three Brand Gulch, when Sloper, having ascended the craggy rims before daylight, descended upon the Three Brand by the back way that Holt had described. Moving cautiously, he worked his way down the long twisting cat trail from above, cocked rifle in hand, eyes and ears alert for signs of far movement or hint of ambush. It took him two hours to reach the Three Brand diggings in this way, and there he found the dead mule mentioned by Holt. The eight-foot location shaft which the state law required was there, and a miscellaneous assortment of picks and drills had been dumped on the ground, together with grub partly ravaged by pack rats and ravens, but at first his limited previous information enabled him to learn nothing of use.

He was weighing in his mind the possibility of Rod Laughlin himself being the center of the Three Brand mystery, when further discovery showed him the injustice of this. In the bottom of the Three Brand shaft, partly covered by returned rubble, Sloper found the body of a man who he instantly knew could be no one but Rod Laughlin. A red stubble of beard he recalled having been mentioned by Holt as characteristic of Laughlin, and a missing finger on the left hand completed the identification by description. Rod Laughlin, foreman for Gideon Holt's Cross Hook, had been shot twice in the back at a distance, and once through the head at close range, and, like Walt Rathbone, he had died with holstered gun.

Farther down the gulch Sloper presently discovered the body of Harry Stucky, disposed as Holt had described, and Stucky he buried with Laughlin in the location shaft that had now, apparently, occasioned the deaths of three men.

Missouri then climbed the trail up which Dundee had gone the night before. A possibility was in his mind that Dundee, perhaps desperately wounded, had disappeared over the rim only to lose his saddle and be left by his horse hurt or dead. Investigation during the night had been impossible; it had become feasible now—at the risk that Dundee, if found alive, would carry out his promise to shoot on sight.

Events were closing sharply about Missouri Sloper. Dundee, taking him for a spy and a hired gunman, had already promised death on sight. A suspicion existed in Moloch that Sloper himself had killed Rathbone, and in Moloch he had defied the law in the person of the deputy who had wished to incarcerate him in the gun-looped jail. And if he were now discovered by Dundee or his men in the cañon in which lay two unaccounted dead, and in which Dundee himself had been wounded from ambush, Missouri's future promised to be both unhappy and sensational.

These things were in his mind as he topped the granite rim over which the wounded Dundee had disappeared, noting the touch of blood where Dundee had gone down, and the scars marking the bolt of Dundee's horse across the rock. He was walking carefully, eyes open and senses alert, yet all at once—Sloper's hand leaped to his gun too late as he stepped from behind a great split of rock to find himself face to face with a rider who sat a horse, motionless as the stone.

What he instantly saw was a rifle that centered on his belt buckle from a range of twenty-five feet, and his gun leaped up. Then, sheepishly, he holstered it again. The rider was Gail Dundee.

"Now, that's what I call jay walking," said the daughter of Andry Dundee. "Good grief, man! You need a guardian. If you're going to walk right into a rider on a horse, what would happen if somebody laid for you in the rocks?"

Missouri grinned. "I guess I'm not used to this sudden death business," he admitted. It was not true that he had taken less precaution than was indicated under the circumstances, but he recognized that a turn of luck had made him look a fool. "Don't miss everything, though. There's a rider coming up the gulch, for instance. He'll show in sight in a couple of minutes. I guess I was listening to that."

"I don't hear any rider," said the girl after a moment.

"He's there, though. But I'm not used to this having enemies on all sides." Sloper was wondering if he should tell about Laughlin and Stucky, but decided to keep his own counsel for the present.

"That's funny, too," she said. "I never saw anybody make enemies any quicker than you. Dad took you for a hired gun, I suppose you know?"

"And did you?" asked Missouri.

"No, but what kind of judge am I? Don't you know that the Tonopah is a pretty hot place for you since you prejudiced Dad?"

"Yes, I know that."

"Then, in heaven's name, why don't you get out?"

"Because I'm a fool."

"Maybe, but is that a reason to get yourself killed by staying here, in the middle of the ugliest scrape . . . ?"

"Staying here is the first thing I've had a good reason for in a long time. I threw away a good job for no reason at all, to come to a place where I wasn't sent for, and sit into a game where I wasn't asked. But . . . I can't lope it now."

"Why?"

The tiny figure of a horseman appeared down-cañon far below. Although the man and horse showed distinctly through the clear mountain air, Gail even yet could hear no sound.

"There's the rider I mentioned. Can you see who it is? I never saw him before."

"Looks like Art Humphreys. *Why* can't you leave?"

"I can't tell you, Miss Dundee."

"Then I'm to understand that my father was right?" The girl's voice sharpened.

"Absolutely not!"

"Then what am I supposed to think?"

"Why do you ask?" he said slowly.

For the first time her steady gray eyes wavered from his own. "I don't know," she admitted.

"But you do."

"But I do?" she insisted sturdily.

"You asked for it," said Sloper, his eyes in the cañon, "and I'm going to give it to you. But I'm sorry, because you won't believe it, and, if you believe it, you won't like it, although after all maybe it don't matter either way."

"That's for me to judge," said Gail Dundee.

"I'll tell you something else first. Do you happen to know that your father has worked his way into a bad hole?"

She hesitated. "Yes, I know that," she admitted.

"I've always thought that Missouri Sloper was pretty good. The other night when I was talking to you, it came to me that I was wrong, and that maybe I was just a saddle bum, after all. And I made up my mind I was going to do one useful thing, if it could be humanly done. I aim to get your father out of this hole."

"You think . . . ?"

"I think I can. And he isn't going to stop me, either, nor you yourself, nor all hell . . . if I get a break."

"But he threatened to kill you!"

"I gathered that."

"Then why?"

"Because I love you, and I loved you from the

114

first minute I saw you ride out of the dust on a palomino horse."

So far as he could see, Gail did not move, or give any sign, but her black horse shifted its hoofs uneasily, as if a sudden obscure message had been communicated through the grip of her knees. The horse fell quiet again, and in the silence Missouri noticed that, although it was of good, even flashy build, it appeared low-headed and worn.

She suddenly flared at him: "What right have you . . . ?"

"You asked me, didn't you?"

"Yes, I asked you," she admitted.

"This whole business will be over in three days, and I'll be out of here. And I won't be bothering you again."

A queer, almost humorous gleam came into Gail's eyes. "In some ways," she said slowly, "you're easily beat."

To her astonishment, his face hardened. "Don't mistake me," he said distinctly. "If I decided to stay in the Tonopah and settle down to get you, I'd get you all right."

By the quick flush of anger that flooded her face, no less than by the quick jerk of her quirt that set her horse to jumping, Sloper thought she was about to lash him across the face. But she cooled instantly.

"You said one true thing, all right," she told him. "You sure think Missouri Sloper's pretty good!"

"Sure I'm good."

"But," she finished, "the Dundees won't be needing any help from you."

If he had an answer, Missouri kept it to himself. He stood rolling a cigarette as she rode off, losing herself in the frozen tumult of the rocks. Then he climbed down into the gulch again to meet Art Humphreys.

"So you're Missouri Scupper," said Humphreys when he had read the note that Holt had left with Missouri.

"Sloper," Missouri corrected. "Though it don't matter."

"Oh. You look like you'd put in a hard night, Missouri."

"I've buried a couple of men . . . and some other stuff."

"Who?"

"Rod Laughlin and Harry Stucky."

Humphreys gave vent to low, bitter cursing, each word distinct, and this lasted more than half a minute. "How shot?" he asked at last.

Sloper told him, and added a short description of the reception party of the night before—omitting, as always, the name of Dundee. "You find anything?"

"Nope, just a plain horse trail, wandering to hell and gone before it traced back to here."

Humphreys went into a silence, during which his eyes perpetually combed the gulch. "Wasn't

116

that Gail Dundee you was talking to up on the rim? What's she doing over here?"

"She didn't say."

"Wasn't that a kind of a chunky black she was riding?"

"With a white blaze," Sloper agreed.

"It's a damned funny thing," said Humphreys moodily. "Don't know as it means much. But I know that horse. And that horse was standing in Moloch the other night when Walt Rathbone was killed."

"In Moloch? Are you sure?"

"Dead certain. He had his hoof over his tie rope as I come by, and I helped him loose. He was the only horse tied near the water trough, and he splashed mud on me as I let his hoof down. Naturally I noticed what horse it was. Why?"

"It explains something Holt noticed over to Dundee's, and nobody there admits riding that horse that night. Well, let it go. This is hell. That horse is going to hang the wrong man . . . if he lives to be hung."

"No."

"No is what I say. Damnation. Why doesn't Elmer Law show with my horse? Somebody's going to eat smoke in Moloch tonight . . . if I get there."

"Smoke? Wind's the wrong way."

"I mean powder smoke!"

117

VII

Elmer Law showed up in the latter part of the morning. Although the Holt ranch lay but eleven miles to the southeast, Elmer had seen no cause for hurry and had saved the horse. Sloper, however, was not annoyed. On cooler thought he had realized that in his present hazardous position it would he safer for him to move about Moloch after dark. The three riders—Sloper, Law, and Humphreys—therefore took their time in riding to Moloch, nineteen miles southwest. And it was dusk—the dusk of Tuesday, June 29th—when the twin stacks of Moloch, weirdly out of place in that vast emptiness of mountain and plain, towered over them at last.

"And who," Sloper was asking Humphreys, "is Dundee's best friend around Moloch?"

Humphreys considered. He always took plenty of time to consider, no matter what the question. He would not have answered promptly if he had been asked his name.

"Dundee hasn't no better friend in the world than Joe Grass, that runs the White Front Hotel. I don't know what Dundee ever done for Joe Grass once. But it must have been something powerful. Joe has always kept a room for him, vacant and ready, and no matter what the rush is in Moloch, or how high a price is being offered for a place to sleep, that Dundee room stands waiting, so if Dundee wants to use it, it's there. Ain't that real friendship for you?"

Missouri swore. "Ain't it?" he repeated sarcastically. "And why wasn't I told this before?"

"I reckon," said Humphreys after some consideration, "because you never asked me."

Sloper studied Humphreys and grinned a sickly grin. Art Humphreys, in spite of the magnificent vocabulary of cuss words that he had acquired, was only a youngster—eighteen at most—with a smooth mild face whose copper tan made his blue eyes look the color of water.

"Elmer," said Missouri Sloper, his voice a growl, "it looks as if maybe, after all, I was wrong and we just been wasting our time."

"I told you we ought to ride on out of here that first night."

"It begins to look like you were right. I've sure missed my cue. We'll just tie up here at the edge and walk in."

"Over by this here trough is a good place," said Humphreys. "It's where the old corral used to be that burned down."

"Is this," Sloper asked, "where you saw that blaze-faced Bar Five horse that night?"

"Yep . . . this is the only street trough in town. Everybody that ties here is supposed to pump a couple of licks. And this is the only mud in town, too . . . so be careful where you step down."

Silently the three walked into Moloch in the thickening dark. They passed a long row of shacks, then came onto the boardwalk that distinguished the heart of the town. Beyond two saloons stood the White Front Hotel, a one-story frame barracks with a two-story false front— devoid of white paint or any other.

"Go in and ask Joe Grass if Dundee was here Saturday night," Sloper told Humphreys.

"That's the night Walt Rathbone was killed?"

"Yes . . . but don't remind him of that. Tell him you saw a horse in town that night that you want to buy, and you want to find out whose it is."

Humphreys vanished quickly. It seemed to the two on the boardwalk that he was gone a long time.

"Grass ain't there," he told them when he reappeared at last.

"Take you all this time to find that out?" demanded Law, exasperated.

"Well, no. His boy was there . . . name of Gus, about fourteen. Said his paw was at the jail, talking to the sheriff."

Sloper whistled.

"What's the matter?" Humphreys asked.

"Mort Six owns the sheriff?"

"He sure does. He pretended to fight him, when he was elected, but everybody knows now that he was a Six man all the time."

"All right. Is that all?"

"Well, I asked the kid about Dundee. The answer was kind of yes and no."

"Yes and no?"

"Yes . . . and no. Gus pulled hisself up like a bantam rooster and told me to go to hell. I worked him over with a few other questions, one at a time, but he denied everything I brung up, including the point that he was a liar. But . . . that kid looked scairt. I think he's holding something back."

Sloper started to go into the White Front but changed his mind. "Can you show me where the window is to that room of Dundee's?"

"Sure."

They ducked between the White Front and the neighboring saloon, and groped through the long black crevice separating the two buildings. At the back the ground sloped away, so that the rear of the hotel was held four or five feet off the ground by a rickety trestling. "There it is," said Humphreys, indicating, the window of the corner room.

"Don't talk so loud," Sloper cautioned him. "All right, Art, you circulate around town and see if you can listen to some reason for Grass being holed up with the sheriff. We'll meet you at the horses."

When Humphreys was gone, Sloper turned swiftly to Law. "Ever try any burglary, Elmer?"

"Very little. I don't know what you're doing, but

I know we'll probably have to shoot our way out if we're caught inside."

"Stand here and keep an eye open. I'm going in."

Sloper turned to the wall of the hotel. A two-by-four stuck out at a convenient height below the window, and this he gripped with his left hand—and stopped.

"Oh, the old son-of-a-gun," he said softly. "Lied and sneaked, and lied. . . ."

"What is it, Missouri?"

Missouri Sloper held out something in the palm of his hand, but Elmer could not see what it was, until Sloper told him.

"Mud," said Missouri. "A hunk of mud, like would stick in the instep of a boot. Here on this step up, under the window."

"Somebody's clumb up there," Elmer deduced.

Missouri snorted. "Somebody that wasn't supposed to be in Moloch, but climbed into this room. Still . . . there's just one more chance."

Sloper ripped off his brush jacket, produced a match, and scaled up to the window. There, with his jacket over his head like a cameraman's hood to hide his match, he made a careful examination of the sill. Then he dropped to the ground again.

"Elmer . . . I take it back . . . I was wrong."

"Cool down, Missouri . . . you're too excitable for a burglar. We got to . . ."

"That window hasn't been opened since the last rain."

"Then the mud . . . ?"

"Nothing but somebody prying around and listening at the window. See what that means?"

"Prob'ly means he was curious about something."

"Don't sprain your head . . . I'll tell you pretty quick. Wait a minute more."

This time, when he had scaled up, Missouri brought the window open with a terrific wrench and disappeared inside. Elmer Law saw the light of a struck match. Then darkness again—and Missouri, shutting the window behind him as he climbed out, vaulted to the ground.

"And what did we steal?" Elmer Law inquired.

"A splinter, Elmer. In my left forefinger, as I struck that match with my left hand, under the washstand edge. We're pretty near caught up with somebody, I think."

"A nice haul," said Elmer. "A hunk of mud and a splinter in your hand. We ought to get a lot of money for this."

"We ought to get the loan of a man's life, is all. Now, by gum, if Art Humphreys hasn't lost himself and got drunk . . ." He led the way back into Moloch's only street.

A scattering of hard-rock and smelter men sauntered along the board walk in twos and threes, with the swagger of men who have put heavy work behind them only to rediscover that they have no place to go. The broad hats of the cowboys drew a glance here and there, but they were not challenged.

"I could use a drink," Elmer grumbled as they passed the last saloon.

"We'll be out of the Tonopah pretty quick," Missouri promised, a sudden weariness in his voice. "Yes, I guess a couple of us have got a drunk coming, all right."

"You don't talk like you was looking forward to it very much."

Missouri tightened his cinch, and Art Humphreys's, too, and, when Elmer had followed his example, they leaned on the hitch rack and waited, while slowly an hour passed.

"We'll go on without him pretty quick," Missouri fumed. "Still . . . I would like to know . . ."

Half an hour more rolled slowly over Moloch, while Elmer squirmed, his nose twitching to the odor of bottled goods from the bars.

Then Art Humphreys came swinging awkwardly down the walk, hurry stretching his stride.

"They've got the dope on him!" he shot out as soon as he recognized the waiting men. "They've broke down Joe Grass!"

"Got the dope on who?"

"Old man Dundee! They've made Grass admit that Dundee was in Moloch Saturday night, and that he quarreled with Walt and made Joe Grass promise not to tell he was here, and . . ."

For once the habitual slow drawl of the youngster was swept away in the excited rush of his news.

"Wait now . . . you're twittering," Elmer Law urged.

"Shut up, Elmer. What else, Art?"

"The whole story that Grass told has got out all over town in about the last twenty minutes. Saturday night Walt Rathbone and Dundee came into the White Front Hotel together, and Dundee asked Grass if Horntoad Holt was in town. When Grass said he was, Dundee said not to tell anybody he was in town, because him and Horntoad had had a falling out, and he didn't want to see him or have anything to do with him for fear he'd lose his temper and there'd be trouble."

"Who'd lose his temper?"

"Dundee'd lose his temper and shoot Holt. And Grass promised not to say anything about it. And he all the more didn't say anything about it after Rathbone was shot. Grass, he didn't like Rathbone anyway, and he thought he'd keep his mouth shut and let good enough alone, but they tricked it out of him."

"What happened that night, according to Grass?"

"Well, Rathbone went out and was gone about an hour, and Grass took some sandwiches back to Dundee's room. Then Rathbone come back, and Grass admits he heard 'em shouting at each other, back there, and, after a while they went out, looking pretty sore and not saying anything. And two deputies has been to Dundee this morning, in a flivver, and asked him was he in Moloch and he said no, and now they know it was a lie, and they've caught him in it, and there's going to be trouble. But all that truck isn't what I started out to tell you."

"Good night, boy. Truck? You don't know anything else as important as that truck, do you?"

"The hell I don't. What I started to tell you is that the sheriff is forming up a big posse in the Horse's Neck saloon, and this damn' town is so dead thirsty for trouble they've got more men than they've got saddles for, pretty near, and the hard-rock men are pouring in there to sign onto the posse without even knowing what it's about, and the sheriff can have an army if he wants, and I'm thinking that, if they get hold of Dundee, they'll make an example of him without ever asking him what he's got to say. And I say it's a hell of a note if the town can put a loop on a cattleman on his range, and I say ride to hell and gather the different brands, and jump their damned posse, and send 'em kiting back. . . ."

"You've got a fine chance, if they're starting tonight." Sloper vaulted into his saddle. "Come on, you Indians!" He whirled his horse and headed back into the town.

"Where you think you're going?" Art demanded, spurring alongside.

"These ponies have come near forty miles today . . . how much farther do you think they'll last? Thirty-five more miles to Dundee's Bar Five?"

"Well, the livery corral is still boarding two of our horses that . . ."

"Livery corral, hell! Where's the garage?"

"That garage feller don't like me," Art Humphreys mourned. "I socked him one last month when . . ."

"Stand by to sock him again," suggested Missouri. He dropped from his horse before an open-faced, lighted shanty wherein an overalled man, head and shoulders under the hood of a weathered car, was jigging the gas feed of a roaring engine.

Sloper had his saddle off, and his bridle over his arm. He slapped his pony's rump, and the tired animal went lumbering off into the dark. There was a certain finality in that move, as if he had burned his bridges behind him. "Now you've done it," said Elmer, raising his voice above the roaring engine in the doorway. "What if this guy won't . . . ?"

"This one sounds pretty good," said Missouri, throwing his saddle into the tonneau of the machine.

The mechanic lifted a face black with grease. "What do you think you're doing?"

"I'll hire this bus," Sloper told him, "to the account of Holt's Cross Hook."

"You will like hell," said the face behind the grease. "I know you drunk cowboys, and I've give you a chance before, and I'll be damned if . . ."

"I'm sorry I haven't got time to explain," said Missouri, lashing out.

The astonished man reeled from the crack of the rider's fist, but recovered and came back, his hands in front of him. Sloper waited, then drove through a long right, with his weight behind it, and this time his man went down.

Sloper walked to the rear of the car and glanced at the tank, which was full, then he slid behind the wheel. "Well, will you get your saddles in here?" he yelled at the others. He meshed the gears with a crash, and the car rolled out of the garage.

Art Humphreys was already on the running board, saddle on his arm and bridle in his teeth.

"Mine's in," said Elmer Law, heaving the leather into the back seat.

"Jump, then!" yelled Sloper. The car shot down the street toward open country.

"You ever drive one of these here before?" Elmer yelled above the roar of the engine.

"I drove a hay truck once," said Missouri. "I put it in the ditch the first day."

"Misery upon misery!" wailed Elmer Law.

The car in which they found themselves was old, her paint long since worn away by the blast of the desert sand, but she was of a heavy breed, and her engine was good. Elmer Law clung to his hat and braced his feet on the instrument board as they careened eastward on the twisting desert trail. Slowly the needle of the speedometer mounted to seventy-five, to eighty, to eighty-five.

"Dundee ain't worth it," said Elmer's wind-whipped voice.

VIII

"Thirty-seven miles," Elmer computed, as they skidded to a stop in front of the long adobe ranch house of the Dundees. "Feller, you've made a fool out of a day's ride in exactly twenty-eight minutes and a half!"

"That gives us plenty of time," commented Missouri. "But there's other motors in Moloch. We've got to persuade Dundee to take himself elsewhere . . . if it can be done."

Light showed in the house, but Dundee was not at home. When, at Missouri's insistence, the three had left their side arms in the car and pounded on the heavy-timbered door, it was Gail Dundee who let them in.

She was very pale, and regarded them with an unfriendly eye, and she did not, at first, put down the rifle in her hands as she backed away from the unbarred door.

"You sure act like you was expecting company," Elmer Law commented. "If ever I get out of the Tonopah without one of these everlasting rifles sticking up right in my face . . ."

Gail disregarded him. "And why this delegation?"

"I want to speak to your father, Miss Dundee," said Missouri soberly.

"He isn't here."

"I'm glad to hear it. I'm right glad to hear it."

"All right. And now you can take yourself out of here."

"I wouldn't have come here without a reason, Miss Dundee. We'll be leaving in a minute. But first you ought to know a couple of things that have happened in Moloch this evening."

She hesitated. "Sit down, then."

They did so, uneasily, and Missouri retailed a compact account of the tricked-out confession of Joe Grass, regarding the presence of Dundee in Moloch the night Rathbone was killed, and of the posse forming in Moloch—perhaps already on the way.

"It's not true," said Gail hotly. "It's not true, a word of it."

"Miss Dundee, if you think I came here to lie to you, I may as well leave, but I tell you that you're tying my hands when you need 'em both."

"I don't mean you," she said more gently. "I mean Joe Grass. After all Dad did for him . . ."

"He was tricked, Miss Dundee, though how I didn't hear."

An instant of puzzlement, of doubt momentarily made her eyes waver. "Do you mean you think . . . ?"

"You've got to believe I mean to help you, Miss Dundee. I know you hate the air I breathe, but you've got to believe in me enough to tell me two things, if ever I'm going to get your father out of this . . . this . . ."

"What do you want to know?"

"Nothing that an innocent man would want to conceal. First, what color horse did your father ride last Thursday?"

"A gray," said Gail. "A little runt of a wild horse gray, just as tough as saddle leather."

"And when he came back Sunday . . . it must have been Sunday?"

"Early in the morning."

"What shape was that gray pony in?"

He could not see that her face changed, but she turned to the wall, putting the rifle back on its pegs.

"I want to know, Miss Dundee, was that pony beat out, and saddle ground, and about half dead?"

She hesitated only an instant more. "And what if he was?" she flamed at him.

In the silence they all heard Art Humphreys whisper to Elmer Law: "You see . . . she even thinks he did it herself."

131

"I'll tell you this," said Gail, talking straight to Missouri. Her voice was low, but trembling with emotion. "If he did, if ever he tells me that he did . . . kill Walt Rathbone . . . I'll know that he had reason enough, and more than enough, and that it was the only thing he could do, and that he shot fair, as fair as ever a man could shoot."

"But he did not shoot him," said Sloper.

Elmer Law stood up, his battered hat dangling in his two hands. "For heaven's sake, why don't you tell her and get it over with? That ridden-out horse she just spoke about is the one last thing that convicts Dundee."

"You fool," said Sloper, "it's the one last thing that clears him."

"And how do you figure that?"

"Have you forgotten the blaze-faced Bar Five horse that Art saw at the water trough that night? And the mud on the step under the window?"

"I don't know anything about what you're talking about," said Art Humphreys slowly. "But if you're depending on Joe Grass telling the truth, I say you're counting on a wind-broke horse."

"I say he told truth enough, and I'm not a bit afraid to gamble my neck that Walt Rathbone got a splinter in his finger where I got mine . . . in Dundee's hotel room."

"Oh, what are you talking about?" Gail cried out, her unnatural self-possession beginning to crack at last.

"I'll tell you what I know," said Missouri, "and what I'm guessing at. Saturday night your father and Walt Rathbone rode into Moloch together. I don't know where they met . . . on the road between here and Rathbone's, it may be. Dundee had persuaded Rathbone to swing with him and sell the Three Brand to Mort Six. They went into the White Front Hotel, and Dundee stayed there, because Holt was in town, and he didn't want trouble, the feeling being pretty bad between those two on the mine question. Rathbone went to close the deal with Mort Six, but Mort Six bucked his price, and Walt got mad and wouldn't close. Rathbone went back to the hotel, and he and Dundee cussed each other out. Then they left . . . Walt to get a drink probably, and your father to ride on home, he being too mad to sleep . . . and still not wanting to tangle with Holt in some saloon."

"Dad didn't drink, anyway," said Gail.

"Well . . . that fits in all the better. No place to go but home. So he rode that gray horse out. Meanwhile, Walt Rathbone was killed in the street."

"But . . ."

"Wait a minute. While Rathbone and your dad were quarreling in that room at the White Front Hotel, somebody was listening at the window."

"Who?" Art demanded.

"Mort Six," said Law.

133

"What could Mort Six learn there that he didn't already know?"

"Who, then?"

Missouri hesitated. "I don't know, but I'm thinking it was a man that rode into town on that blaze-faced black horse. It was the only horse tied near the water trough at about that time, and right at that water trough is the only mud in Moloch that a man would be likely to run into in the street."

Elmer broke in: "Now, do you know for sure that somebody else hadn't come by that trough and give the pump a lick, and picked up some mud? Or that that mud hasn't been there ever since the hotel was built, in this dry climate? Or that the mud wasn't picked up back of the restaurant kitchen where they throw the dishwater out? Or that it wasn't some drunk climbed up to that window looking for a free place to sleep? Or that the black horse wasn't ridden in by some Dundee cowboy that got overpowering thirsty for a drink?"

"I don't know any of them things," Missouri admitted.

"And I never seen such a thin case in my life," said Elmer Law. "Why would anybody go listening at that window, even if he did? And why come in on a Bar Five horse to do it? And how does that hook up with killing Harry Stucky and Rod Laughlin?"

134

"Rod . . . is he . . . ?" Gail cried out.

"I thought your father would have told you," said Missouri. "Somebody's got Rod Laughlin, and Harry Stucky, too, over at the Three Brand Gulch. I could have told you yesterday, but . . . I was hoping to find out more about it before the news got out."

"Oh, poor Rod."

"You knew Rod pretty well?"

"He came to see me oftener than anybody else, I suppose, and he was always bringing me something funny and useless . . . an armadillo, or a tortoise egg, or some crazy little thing." The tears were in her eyes as she added: "I expect I liked Rod better than any . . . anybody in the Tonopah."

"One link more," said Missouri curiously.

"You still building up a case?" said Elmer pityingly. "Found the sinister Chinaman yet? Of all the far-fetched . . ."

"Did you ever trail deer," said Missouri, "and come to hard ground? And pretty soon you found where just a little pebble or two was kicked aside . . . and there could be a thousand explanations for that . . . but you went on, and finally the trail got clear again, and you found out you was right all the time?"

"Horse feathers," said Elmer.

"I know only one way to work on a thing like this," said Missouri, "and that is to collect up the peculiar things . . . the little things that don't fit in with the ordinary way people act. They all point to something. One of them is pretty apt to point right. And when two things point the same way, and that way is into the dark . . ."

"Why, then, a sensible feller turns right around and goes back," said Elmer. "And now, I suppose . . ."

"And now, if you don't mind," said Missouri, "I'll ask you fellers to let me speak to Miss Dundee alone."

"But . . . ," began Gail, and fell silent.

"Pick the three best horses in the corral," Sloper ordered, "and put our saddles on them."

"You can't do that," Gail said.

"We have to. Now move, damn it, you two," Missouri snapped at them. "We've wasted time enough."

When they had gone out, Missouri kicked the door shut behind them with his heel, and strode across the room to Gail. She got up nervously, and he stood looking down at her.

"You don't trust me much, do you?" he said at last.

"Why should I?" she asked sharply.

"I was hoping you would have an answer to that."

"I think you're somebody that came here without being sent for, and sat in other people's game without being asked, and the sooner you leave other people's business alone the better."

"Almost my very own words," Missouri pondered.

"And they fit."

Suddenly his hands shot out and caught her wrists in a grip like that of wolf traps, forcing her to stand close to him. "Now, you look at me!" he commanded so savagely that for a moment she was silenced. "I've come to a place where I can't go any further without your help . . . yet, if your father is to be saved, I have to ride now, at once . . . you hear. Now answer my questions . . . be quick! Where's those two cowboys your father signaled in the night I was here?"

"He changed his mind and sent them back to their work on the north range."

"Where's that Indian boy, and the cook?"

"Both quit today."

"Where's Al Closson?"

"Fired last night."

"Why?"

"Because Dad didn't trust him." Her answers were coming quickly now, her voice gaining an almost hysterical quality from the urgency of his own.

"And where's Lou Stam?"

"He went with Dad . . . he's the only one Dad counts on any more."

"And where is your father?"

"I won't tell you!" She made a sudden effort to free her wrists from his grasp, but could not, and stood, half turned, watching him, fascinated, like a wildcat come upon in a trap.

"You little fool. There's no time to waste. Your father must be warned."

"But . . ."

"Do you think there'll be any sense or justice in a Moloch posse? It'll be a plain mob, half drunk and on the running hunt. I've got reason to know those Moloch mobs . . . and, if you think there'll be any mercy in a gang out of the sulphur smoke of Moloch, why . . ."

"I know all that."

"Do you think they'll need to know who they're hunting, or why, or anything about it? Do you think . . . ?"

"Let me go, then. I tell you, I'll warn him myself."

"And I tell you that you'll not!" His voice rose angrily, bearing down her will. "I know Andry Dundee's type . . . I've seen it a thousand times . . . and I know what he'll do. He'll barricade and fight to the last cartridge. Do you suppose he wants you there? Do you want to see him walk out and give himself up to that mob, to save you from the danger of gunfire?"

"I'd never let him. . . ."

"You couldn't stop him . . . and you know it. Now gamble, if you're going to . . . once and for all . . . your father's life on whether I lied to you on the rim of Los Muertos. Where is Andry Dundee?"

"At Black Gulch."

He dropped her hands instantly, and she swayed as if she would fall, but caught the back of a chair.

"Now get your six-gun and blanket roll and go sleep in the sage," he ordered her. "And don't let that hell pack from Moloch find you here, either."

He was outside, running toward the corral. "Throw down those bars! Haze those ponies out!"

"What's the idea?" shouted Elmer Law.

"If that posse comes this far by motor, I want them to get no horses here. Action, now!"

Art Humphreys handed Missouri his gun belt as he mounted the horse they had saddled for him. Hazing half a dozen ponies from the corral ahead of them, to blur out the sign that would tell the hunt which way they had gone, the three riders struck to the west, where rose the black hulks of the Warbonnets, blotting out the horizon stars.

IX

"What you fellers don't realize," said Elmer Law, "is that I ain't et since daybreak."

"What about that can of beans at the Three Brand Gulch?"

"Oh, am I supposed to count a little can of beans?"

They fell silent, plodding on, close now to the foot of the great Warbonnet range. They had come twelve miles, and they had almost reached their destination, but, because they had come slowly, walking their horses, the night was almost gone. With Dundee where he was, they had time enough.

In the first gray light of dawn the horses walked up the long slope of the alluvial fan that reached out into the desert from the mouth of Black Gulch—a spread of sand and gravel augmented spring by spring, as the promised water of the Tonopah rushed down from the mountains to lose itself under the sand.

"The soddy, where I figure he'll be at," said Art Humphreys, "is over to the side, on a ledge. It ain't Andry Dundee's exactly. The ranchers in the south valley put it up, because there's a stretch of good deer country above, and they used to make a stopover of it so regular that they kind of built a soddy to stop at."

"Any cows run up there with the deer?"

"Only the longest-horned ones figure they can climb it."

Art Humphreys pulled up his horse, and they waited a few minutes, lounging in their saddles, for the light to increase. They had more than one obvious reason for not wishing to approach Dundee in bad light.

Twenty minutes later they advanced to where, on a slanted ledge of rock continuous with the drift, a crumbling soddy squatted, backed up hard against a 400-foot wall of granite, and looking mighty small, and trivial, in the first cold light.

They halted their horses at a distance, and Sloper, having hung his gun belt on his saddle horn, walked on alone.

Andry Dundee came to the door while Sloper was still at twenty yards and the inevitable rifle that seemed the badge of the Tonopah was in his hands. Sloper recalled the skirmish at Three Brand Gulch as he saw that Dundee was favoring one stiff, almost useless leg.

"I been watching you come up," said the old man, his eyes narrowed as if he could not clearly see Sloper—but knew him all the same. "I been watching you quite a ways, and I like your guts."

"Glad to hear you like something, Dundee."

"You remember what I told you about next time I sighted you in the Tonopah? All right . . . where's your gun?"

"Dundee, my gun's on my saddle."

"Dog yellow, huh? And who's that behind you? Two Holt men, I suppose?"

"You can call them that."

"All right, then . . . we understand each other, Sloper. Now, you just turn right around and hightail back to that horse of yours . . . which looks a whole hell of a lot like a horse of mine, by the way! . . . and you straddle him, and you git! And if you swerve or make a break toward the gulch, I swear I pick off no less than three!"

"Dundee," said Missouri Sloper, "I know well enough you don't like me, and heaven knows I've got little reason to like you. Put it that I'm doing for you what I'd do for any man that's come under an injustice. I come here to speak my piece, and I'll speak it. And you can believe what I say or not, and act accordingly or contrary, and in any case, after that, you can go to hell and be damned to you, for I've done what I could."

"Why, you infernal pup, I'll . . ."

"I've come from Moloch, by way of your place, and I'm here by the good sense of your daughter, who . . ."

"What! Look here, Sloper, you mean to tell me she's still at the Bar Five?"

"I told her to go take her blankets out in the sage. But she was there when I come by."

"Why, that daw-gone little . . . why, I told her to ride to Rathbone's and stay there until I come."

"I supposed you'd made some such provision. Now I'm telling you about what they're doing in Moloch. I rode in there at sundown, and out within two hours, but during that time Joe Grass spilled the beans on you, and it's known you were in Moloch when Walt Rathbone was killed, and that you quarreled with him. I wouldn't blame Grass if I was you. Others must have seen you as you rode in, and they crossed him up most likely. A sheriff's posse is formed to take you for murder. I think they aimed to ride last night. There'll be good and plenty men, and, if a Moloch mob is your idea of an arm of justice, just stick around, Mister Dundee. Just who-all is back of this sudden wave of righteous indignation, you probably know better than me, but I'd say it must be somebody pretty significant."

"I know, all right."

"I suppose you think it's Holt, but I can tell you . . ."

"It ain't Holt," said Dundee.

"All right. Now I've told you what I know, and you ought to know what's good for you, and good bye, and to hell with you," said Missouri Sloper.

"And just where did *you* get dealt into this?" demanded Dundee.

"I seem to have turned out to be a saddle bum and a meddler," Sloper told him, "which same is a break for you, and I frankly hope it'll be appreciated someday by your daughter . . . who, by the way, you don't seem to know how to take care of very good."

"And you're another, I suppose, that thinks you could take care of her better," snarled Dundee.

"No, I realize she's not for any saddle bum, Dundee."

"You mean that?"

"I'm pulling out of the Tonopah . . . if that's what you want to know."

"You got more sense than most, at that," said Dundee wearily, and for a moment something like a grim twinkle creased his morning-red eyes. "Well, call in your friends if you can vouch for 'em. There's breakfast to think of, and a thing or two I want to ask you."

"I don't know as we choose any . . ."

"Don't get proud with me, cowboy. I'm willing to admit I seem to have had you wrong. If you don't want anything to eat, your partner does. What's his name . . . John Law?"

"Elmer."

"Elmer. And one of the most proficient eaters ever I seen. Send him in, and, if you want to stand outside in dignified insultedness, you kin."

Missouri grinned, and weakened. "I guess you're right, Dundee." They shook hands for the first time.

When Elmer and Art Humphreys had been waved in, the four men regarded each other somberly through the smoke of frying bacon.

"And where's Lou Stam?" asked Sloper.

"I sent him to Moloch yesterday, to reconnoiter. Oh, I've seen this coming a mile. Ike Trumbull was up at my place the Monday after Walt was gunned. Ike has the Box Bar, down to the south of Holt. He'd heard talk in Moloch then already. I come in from . . . I come in that night, it was the night after you were at my place, and Ike had plenty to say. Everybody knows now who killed Walt Rathbone, of course, and . . ."

"Excepting me, maybe," Sloper said.

"You mean to say Holt hasn't figured it out?"

"I can't answer for Holt," Sloper decided after a moment.

"I'll tell you then. Mort Six killed Walt Rathbone. He was sore because Rathbone turned him down on his mine offer at the last minute. It's common talk that Mort Six has his back to the wall and stands to lose smelter and all. So when Walt kicked the traces, that was too much."

"How do you know this, Dundee?"

"Who else had as good a reason? And it's Mort Six is putting his bought-and-paid-for sheriff on me now."

"And what's his reason for that? Didn't you hold out to sell the Three Brand to him?"

"I sure did. I blame myself now. Sell we should have, but never to him. What Mort Six didn't count on was the way the Tonopah would rise up against him. He's been the best-hated man in the Tonopah since his stacks went up, for more reasons than one, and now that he's gunned Walt, he's gone too far. Ike Trumbull's fighting mad, and with Ike there's Gill Meade, that has the Two Diamond, and Ad Clarke of the Circle Bob . . . powerful men, as power goes in a desert. And always old Horntoad Holt. Oh, Mort Six is done for all right."

"But this play at you . . . ?"

"This play at me is his last one . . . a try at stirring up a dust, and throwing a bait to the wolves. But the cattlemen see through him to the man, and it's only his pick-axe gorillas that he can do anything with . . . and even they pretty near burned him out two months back."

"But just the same, Dundee, if that posse ever lays hands . . ."

"Me? I'll slip through his fingers. He thinks I'll stand and fight, and never live to tell the tale nor speak for myself. I won't. I've been waiting for this posse. They'll come by way of my ranch, and from here I can see them most of the way. I'll be up in the deer and goat country by the time they hit. Look eastward. If they'd so much as reached the ranch house, you'd see the dust across the twelve miles, though the house is hid by the dip. We got time to talk it over, you see."

"And after that?"

"It won't be long. The old fox will be out of the hills in time to see Mort Six hung. And then down comes them damned smokestacks, and what's left of Moloch will be his narrow-gauge railway . . . which we can put to good use."

Dundee grinned twistedly and filled his mouth with bacon. Old Andry, Sloper thought, was plenty sure of himself, all right.

"And what's your opinion," asked Sloper, "of the killing of Laughlin . . . and Stucky?"

Dundee stopped chewing and for a long moment he regarded Sloper. Yet, because Dundee's back was to the light, Sloper could not be sure that his face changed in any way. "Oh, you was over there?"

"Yes, I was there," Sloper admitted. Gail, then, had not mentioned seeing him there, which was curious, but not as curious as the fact that Dundee had not told his daughter of what he had found.

Elmer Law, who had been watching Dundee in profile, went to the stove for more coffee—and from behind Dundee's back made three quick words in sign language with his hands. *Guilty . . . guilty . . . guilty,* Elmer Law's hands insisted. Without knowing much sign language, Sloper still recognized that. He shook his head.

"Somebody took a shot at me over there, too, and give me this game leg," said Dundee, resuming his mastication.

"Yes, I saw that, too," said Sloper. "Though I didn't see who."

Once more Dundee studied Sloper for a long moment. Then he banged his cup down with exasperation. "Damned if I understand your game, Sloper!"

"Right or wrong, at least you're Gail's father . . . that's my platform, Dundee," said Sloper slowly.

"I suppose that's all a man can expect from a stranger," said Dundee glumly. "At that, it's a hell of a lot more than I asked."

"What's your idea of those killings?"

"Mort Six again," said Dundee promptly. "It's

his aim to make the Three Brand title lapse on that claim . . . then jump it. I guess you know that, if assessment work wasn't started by noon tomorrow . . . it's the Thirtieth, isn't it? . . . the present owners are disqualified. He'll run into Holt there, though. Holt knows, by this time, that Rod's dead and the work isn't done?"

"He knows."

"I was counting on that. Had to count on it . . . being shagged into the sticks myself, like any herd-busting Sonora yak. By thunder, it's something to swallow, you know? But he'll pay for it to the hilt. I should have been shot the day I put in a word for his damned proposition."

"You might be yet," mumbled Elmer Law, too long suppressed.

"What's that?"

"I didn't say nothing, Mister Dundee."

Dundee stood up abruptly. "Now you jiggers look here. I've swallered you fellers . . . and it was a hell of a stretch, too . . . but I've taken you at your spoken word here, and I'm damned if I mean to wash down a whole string of insinuations."

"If it's me you're shouting at," said Elmer, his voice unexpectedly going down to an ugly soft drawl, "you can save it. I ain't rode all night for your benefit to have you . . ."

"Feller, I didn't ask you here . . . nor anything from you in any way . . . and I . . ."

"Did you ever think," said Elmer in that soft

lethal drawl, "that you might be liable to fall into something else you didn't ask for, running off your mouth that way?"

"Shut your head, Elmer," Missouri snapped.

"I'll take a whole lot from a man I like," Law said, disregarding him, "and maybe that gets me took wrong sometimes. But, by the great almighty hell in the foothills"—he came to his feet, and his voice rose at last—"I don't aim to be chawed and swallered and spit up and trampled on by no blowed-up old reprobate just because he's got a pretty daughter. . . ."

The veins stood purple on Dundee's forehead. "You keep that kid's name out of your mouth, or by . . ."

"A pretty daughter that you've run off and left while you skedaddled for the timber!"

"Hold it, Dundee!" Missouri ripped out.

The old man's hand froze on his pistol butt as Missouri clicked back the hammer of his six-gun, already out and leveled, at rest, across the table. Words could not have stopped Dundee's draw, but that familiar *click* of the cocking hammer accomplished what the voice could not.

"Drop that gun back where you got it, Elmer," said Missouri. "You can't pop him while I got him covered, very well."

"Get out of this, Sloper," Elmer Law raved. "I'll bet my last cent the old miscreant is at the bottom of every murder in the Tonopah, and I stand ready

149

to back that, and give him an even break of it right here."

"What a hot theory that is," said Sloper. "For why should he want to lapse his own share in the Three Brand by killing Rod Laughlin?"

"It's a theory beats yours," growled Elmer. "Am I the only one has to have reasons for what I think?" Sulkily he let his gun drop back into its leather.

"I'm still watching you, Dundee," Sloper mentioned.

"You might as well come out with your game first as last," Dundee rasped at him. "Partner blew up on you, did he? Just as you pretty near learned something, huh? Oh, you're a cute one, all right."

"You see?" said Elmer.

"See yourself," rumbled Sloper. "Dundee, like it or not, I'm in this thing now, and I'm going to stay in it till it settles, one way or the other. And if you two fancy gun fanners will let it lay long enough to . . ."

"You can talk pretty big from the look-out seat," said Dundee, his voice quivering, "but holster that gun, and three to one, or six, I'd as lief . . ."

"Don't go too far with me, Dundee."

"He'll go as far as he likes," said Elmer. "Ain't he behind his daughter's skirts?"

The guns of Law and Dundee whipped out together, the threat of Sloper's gun forgotten. Yet neither fired, for Dundee, even as he went for his weapon, had whirled to the door. They learned afterward that he never heard that last taunt of Elmer Law's.

Up the long slope of the alluvial fan came a hard-running horse, marbled with lather, and wheezing out great snorting grunts at every laboring jump. Yet, as he approached the three horses from the Bar Five, the rider dragged his half blind horse to a stop and put up both hands.

"Al Closson!" exclaimed Dundee. "Now what the devil . . . ?"

Closson dropped from his horse, gathered with difficulty the now dragging reins of the three standing horses, and came on afoot at a run, leading all four.

"Help me get the jugheads in," he gibbered, dragging his own dead-beat horse through the door. "They're already on us!"

"Who is?" demanded Dundee. "What's the matter with—"

"The posse, you old fool!" Closson shouted at him. "They never went to the Bar Five at all . . . God knows how they knew to come straight here. Great grief, we ain't got so much as a window or a rat hole to shoot through!"

"You crazy?" said Dundee, his eyes starting. "It ain't possible that . . ."

"Look, if you think it ain't!"

From out of sight beyond the bulge of a spur came a rider, perhaps 500 yards away, then a second, then three together. Closson's gun crashed from the doorway, and dust jumped in front of the first horseman. The leading horse brought up on his haunches, and all five turned and cut back to shelter but not until two more had shown themselves, suggesting unknown numbers to come.

Within the little soddy the four horses and the five men made an overwhelming crush.

"And a sweet mess this is," said Elmer Law. "What about giving that bunch a rush?"

"Rush thirty-one men?" said Closson.

"A bust up the gulch is our cue," said Dundee.

"I knew it!" said Closson. "That's why I had to get here. They've thought of that last night already, and split the posse, and part of 'em rode all night to get that way cut off. They're sifted all along the rim by now."

"Hell's whistles," said Elmer, "a straight ride of it is better than cooped up like fifty sheep in a box stall."

"Riding double?" said Closson pointedly. "I bet old foxy Dundee has hid his horse a half mile up that gulch. Yeah? I thought so. I started to tell him some sense last night, and he fired me. He thinks he's an old-time Indian scout or something."

"Not sore at him," Elmer suggested to Dundee. "Here's another easy mark trying to get shot in your favor."

"No," said Dundee mournfully. "I'm took down

a peg this time. So this is the feller I fired, is it? Maybe," he admitted wearily, "I ain't going to turn out the good judge of men I thought I was."

"No," said Elmer, "you ain't."

A bullet chugged into the outer adobe.

"Rifles over beyond, in the rock dump already," grunted Sloper, getting his gun belt from his saddle. "Well, we've got a nice safe hole-up, at that."

"Lovely," said Elmer brightly. "Horses to eat, and everything except room enough to set down."

"And no loopholes," said Closson.

"That's easy fixed." Sloper, after a glance at the board roof, dragged the axe-built table to the wall. He stepped up on this, and smashed out some of the dry-rotted boards of the roof with his fist. Through the aperture he took a shot at some target unseen, and was answered by an ill-aimed volley. He stepped down again.

"Get one?" asked Elmer.

"Two," said Sloper. "Do you think I'm just wasting my time?"

"Come night we'll make a rush," said Dundee gloomily, "and get clear easy enough, most likely."

"And which of us is going to flee for life on foot?" Elmer wanted to know. "We're still shy a horse, you know."

"What's left of us by then will have plenty pick of horses," Al Closson predicted.

"I'll go up the mountain afoot . . . easy in the dark," said Dundee.

Missouri said: "We'll draw lots for that."

"How they made such a clean guess where I'd be beats me."

"They didn't find out from me," said Closson emphatically.

"And where's Lou Stam?" Sloper asked Closson.

"Dead, I guess."

"Dead? Great grief, another?"

"I saw him in Moloch, but didn't talk to him, being sore at the outfit from being fired. But I know that last night he got a horse from the livery corral and lit out about seven o'clock. He couldn't've got far, because within the hour his horse was back at the corral, saddle and all, and the saddle all bloody. And the horse was pretty steamy, and bleeding at the nose."

"Have they found Lou yet?"

"Not that I know. I left about midnight, after I heard about the split posse aiming to cut off Black Gulch behind you. I rode right on top of the posse in the dark, and joined 'em and rode with 'em. Just before daylight, I begun pulling out ahead, but not soon enough . . . they sighted me and caught on. What a goat my pony turned out to be. Moloch is stripped of decent horses."

That was all Closson knew. After that they waited, contenting themselves as best they could there in the close steam of the ponies, while the day dragged by. Sometimes a rifle or two spoke, out beyond, and bullets chugged in the adobe, but there was no attack, and without action the day stretched long.

Sloper took time to learn what he could from Dundee. It was little enough. Dundee admitted now that he had been in Moloch Saturday night. But, beyond confirming the statements of Joe Grass, he contributed nothing of value.

Just at dusk a blazing torch sailed in an arc and fell in the doorway. Elmer hooked it in and stamped it out, while the horses shouldered and trampled within the close walls, but a second torch was better aimed, falling within twenty feet of the door, but out of reach. Someone of the attackers had wormed his way to a protecting rock very close, from which point he could keep torches going to light their way of escape. Sloper located the torch thrower, and tried a few ricochets without effect, and after that a sobered council whispered within the crumbling adobe on the ledge.

"Boys," said Dundee—and his voice was that of an aged man—"boys, I've been a fool. From start to finish I've been stubborn and all-fired salty and a fool. I see now where I've prejudiced most of the fellers that wanted to be my friends, and bucked everybody, and little thanks has anybody got that's tried to help me. And it's my fault that you all are here tonight. And now I got just one right in this world left, but it's a right I'll fight for, same as I've always fought to have my own way. I'm going first through that door."

"You won't go three . . . ," began Elmer.

"That's as may be," said Dundee. "Will anybody trade a second Colt for my rifle?"

"I reckon," said Al Closson slowly, after a silence.

"Then give it here, son, and I'll get going."

"Now wait a minute," said Sloper. He was thinking first, last, and always of his brash promise to Gail Dundee.

"And what have you got to say about it?" Al Closson demanded unexpectedly.

"I happen to be going out first myself," Sloper said.

"You are like hell," said Elmer. "Who elected you the bull with the brass collar?"

"Let Dundee have his pick," Art Humphreys said.

Missouri Sloper did some fast thinking. After all, the first man out, with the right horse, would have the benefit of surprise—and benefits were going to be scarce. "All right," he conceded.

He turned to the crowded horses and began wheeling out the horse Elmer had ridden from the Bar Five Ranch. By a curious chance it was the same palomino upon which he had first seen Gail Dundee, and it brought the picture of her into his mind again with a sudden poignancy. It was funny how even now his mind was so full of Gail—Gail Dundee.

Palominos made soft horses, but sometimes they could run, and Missouri judged this one to be the best of the four. He had noticed its long, clean, easy stride. "Get up on the step, Elmer, and get ready to give him a covering fire. Don't stir them up, though, until they've already begun pasting us." He was groping to put the reins of the palomino into Dundee's hand.

"You ready to follow?" asked Dundee.

"Wait," said Closson. "Leave that last torch die down some."

Closson and Humphreys got to their horses' heads. One of them sidled a pony against the table where Elmer stood, waiting to fire, and Elmer passed an arm through the loop of the rein.

"Now," said Closson.

"If you get clear," said Dundee, "try for the Bar Five. You can hold them forever there. But, Art . . . you there, Art?"

"Yes, sir."

"Art, ride south and take word to Ike Trumbull. He'll know what to do, and he won't be long." Dundee's voice sounded curiously faint and far away. "Every rider on the range will rally to you . . . if you make it through. I guess I don't need to tell you all to look out for Gail." His guns cocked—a double *click*.

At that moment a new torch spun in a parabola

from the hide-out of the watcher in front, and for a moment Missouri saw Dundee in the doorway, looking curiously straight and young in the light of the fresh flare.

"Get back a second, Dundee," Sloper hissed. He was pressing forward the palomino horse. "Here's your . . . for God's sake, wait!"

Unhurriedly Dundee had stepped out into the full light of the flare.

A gun crashed from the position of the watcher in the rocks, and both Dundee's guns answered. From one of the holes Sloper had knocked in the roof Elmer fired, deliberate and slow, once and twice more, while the rifles woke beyond, and within the horses jigged, clattering their hoofs on the rock floor.

Missouri had leaped to the door, and his gun was lashing out past the tall, unhurried figure of Dundee, now almost at the flame of the torch itself. Then Dundee staggered, fired once more uncertainly, and pitched face downward, his hat rolling from his head.

"Git out of the way!" Art Humphreys snarled at Sloper. Now that they had begun their rush, it was all important that they jam it through without delay, yet for a moment Missouri stood like a man out on his feet, his eyes on the fallen form of Dundee.

Suddenly Dundee moved, and Sloper saw him reaching forward with one claw-like, horribly

158

shaking hand. The hand gripped the torch in the heart of its flame, and the red light snuffed out as it was drawn in and crushed under the body of the fallen man. It was the last move of Andry Dundee—but by it he had given the rest their lives.

Somebody snatched Sloper back out of the doorway. A sudden shouldering of 800 pounds of horseflesh bunted him aside, and Art Humphreys, low on his pony's neck to clear the doorway, drove out into the starlight. Sloper heard Art gasp as his knee jammed crushingly against the side of the door, then the *thud* of the running hoofs was lost in the rattle of the besiegers' guns.

"Elmer got that fire thrower," said Closson, already in the saddle. "Come on, you!"

He rushed his horse through the door. Sloper caught a glimpse of him as he spurred recklessly over the break of the ledge, reins swinging free from the horn as the rifle in his hands spat red flashes in the dark.

"Let's go, you damned fool!" said Elmer.

"I'll be coming," said Missouri. "Good bye, then. See you in the penitentiary. . . ."

He was gone, his horse leaping unnecessarily high over the body of Dundee. Elmer was not firing. Sloper guessed he was trying to reload as he rode.

Last of all Missouri Sloper came out, not at the gallop, but walking that pale palomino horse. He swung low out of the saddle to grope for the body of Dundee. The horse was taller than he had expected, and he had to lose his left stirrup and hook his spur on the cantle in order to reach the ground. The horse shied, nearly throwing him, as he hoisted Dundee's 170 pounds by the belt, but he got his burden across the saddle at last, and under the spur the palomino bolted after the rest.

X

Owing to the darkness and the disorganization of the posse, the chase proved short. One Moloch man, it was later learned, shot another through the arm, and another killed a Moloch horse from behind, but after the death of Dundee, who in his last moment had managed to extinguish the give-away torch, none of the party from the soddy was touched.

Sloper eased down the palomino, as the sound of pursuit tangled and died away behind. Walking his horse under its double burden, it took him until nearly midnight to find the Dundee ranch house, after nearly passing it in the tricky light of the stars. No lights showed in the house, but the glow of cigarettes guided him to the corral.

"Well, for gosh sake," said Elmer Law, "we thought we was rid of you . . . we all agreed you'd been downed without firing a shot."

"I took my time," Sloper admitted

"What you got there?"

"Nothing you don't know about already."

They stood silently, as he eased Dundee's form to the ground.

"I'm glad Gail ain't here," said Closson at last. "You been so long coming we already took that car you borried and run her clear over to Rathbone's, twenty miles, I guess . . . and left her there and come back again."

"She was here, was she?"

"She come in out of the brush, scouting us up, and recognized us before she come out in the open."

"Does she know her father . . . ?"

"Yes, she knows. It's a wonder we didn't tell her you was dead, too, but she was so broken up we didn't get to it."

"I wish to heaven you had," said Sloper. "Still, it don't matter. Was she torn up pretty bad by the news?"

"Pretty bad, Missouri. But she was steady enough by the time we turned her over to Missus Rathbone."

"Do you know if Art Humphreys got away?"

"Pretty sure he did. He probably followed out Dundee's orders, and is rousing up the whole darn' range."

"Wasted effort. I don't think Moloch'll bother much more."

"No, these righteousness manhunts generally peter out when their liquor goes cold on them."

"Elmer and I ought to go back and report to Holt, by rights," Missouri supposed.

"Go ahead," said Closson. "I'll stay here. There'll be a pile of riders accumulating here in the course of tomorrow, if Art Humphreys wasn't hit and gets to the Box Bar. They can turn a hand to helping dig a hole. She'd want him out here under the pepper trees, I suppose?"

"I guess."

When they had carried Dundee into the house, and found feed for the ponies they had used, Elmer Law and Missouri Sloper struck southward in the car that had brought them from Moloch. It was well toward morning when Sloper pulled up at the Holt ranch, dull-eyed and weary, with Elmer snoring in the back seat.

Holt was not on the place. Worn out and careless of the future, Sloper flung himself on Holt's bunk and slept. The sun was two hours high when he was awakened by the exhaust of a second car pulling up in front of Holt's ramshackle dwelling. Sloper came to his feet, instinctively hitching his gun belt into place, as the doorway darkened.

Solid in the doorway, red-eyed, haggard, and gray, stood Morton Six.

The two men looked at each other, hostile but noncommittal, for a long moment. "Looking for Holt?"

Six nodded.

"I don't know where he is. Hardly looked for you here, Six."

"I suppose not. Expecting Holt back?"

"Couldn't say."

"He's dead some place. I wouldn't doubt. What a nightmare of a week. Man after man . . ."

"Your posse got Dundee, I guess you know?"

"So I heard this morning. I'd give anything on earth," said Mort Six in a dead voice, "to have Dundee's life back."

"You figure me to believe that?"

"I don't care whether you do or not. Dundee was the wrong man."

"And how did you find that out?"

Six shrugged. "What's the difference now?"

"If there's one thing left around here that I'm interested in," said Missouri Sloper, "it's in clearing Dundee's name for his daughter's sake. That means the rope for someone, and I, for one, don't care much who."

"Interested in the Dundee girl, are you?" asked Six abruptly. Sloper did not reply. "Maybe you're interested in saving her share of the Three Brand copper, then."

"So now we come to the point of this little call," said Sloper dryly. "And what's your proposition now?"

"No proposition. The Three Brand outfit stands to lose its claim if the assessment work isn't begun before noon, is all. I've just found out that the assessment work hasn't been done, and why, and that a party of fifteen men . . . maybe more . . . will take over the diggings at twelve oh one."

"What's this . . . a challenge?"

"No . . . I'm out of the Tonopah, Sloper."

"Smelter and all?"

"Bankrupt to the last dime. It isn't that I'm caring about. I wasn't back of that mob that got Dundee, by the way. I put the sheriff on him because I thought he was guilty, but the mob was raised by somebody else, who, together with the mob, forced the sheriff's hand. And not out of spite against Dundee, either."

"What then?"

"This morning the word is leaking out that the Three Brand will be open to re-staking, and Moloch is just waking up to it. With the exception of fifteen horses that have been set aside for this purpose, there's not a horse in Moloch. Every last one of any account is at Black Gulch. By the time the town has scoured horses from the range, it'll be too late, and the few picked men that are in on the deal will have scooped Los Muertos copper."

"You mean to say that Dundee was snuffed out just to use up Moloch horses?"

"I don't ask you to believe it, or care a hoot whether you do or not. It's the truth, though, as it happens. Inconceivable, is it? I'll tell you this . . .

I can buy any man's life in the Tonopah for five hundred dollars . . . let alone a million."

"I don't doubt you have ways," said Sloper. "And yet . . . you mean to make me think that you're letting slip the Three Brand copper?"

"Damn the Three Brand copper, and damn the day it was discovered." Slowly, as he spoke, there was more passion in his voice than Sloper had believed was in the man. "I've given you your tip. It's your chance to save the Dundee girl's property, if you're interested in that. I meant to bring the word to Holt. I can't wait for him. Do what you like."

"What are you suggesting?"

"Ride like hell for your ranchers, borrow every cowboy on the range, swarm into Three Brand Gulch, start the assessment work with your range outfits to stand off the Moloch men. . . ." For just a moment a faint spark of executive power had returned to Mort Six's eye, but it died at once. "Or what you like. It's nothing to me." He turned back to his car.

"I'd like to know a couple of other things from you," Sloper said.

"You want to know who the killer is, don't you?" said Mort Six. "Think you ever will?" Seated behind his wheel he surveyed Sloper with a weary eye. "You're wasting your time, Sloper. You'll have your hands full today, if you save the Three Brand Mine, and after that . . . no, I

don't think you'll have your hands on him again."
Mort Six smiled wanly.

Sloper came forward to the running board. "And where have I seen you before?" he asked curiously.

"I'm sure I don't know . . . or care."

"I'm wondering," said Sloper slowly, "if I wouldn't get me a killer if I plugged you where you sit?"

"Go ahead, if you think that will clear anything up. No, it isn't so easy as that, my boy."

Sloper stood back as the car pulled out, sluggish in the sand. Elmer Law was sitting up in the back seat of their borrowed car. He had, Sloper learned, heard the tail end of the conversation.

"There goes a crazy man, Missouri."

"There's something wrong with him all right. Ever see him before, Elmer? Any other place, I mean?"

"He kind of looks familiar, all right . . . now that you speak of it. Most fellers do. You going to lead a fight for the Three Brand lode?"

Sloper shook his head. "Six has a funny idea of distances, if he thinks his suggestion would work. Even with Art Humphreys doing a Paul Revere all night, there won't be much of anybody to collect at the Bar Five until late afternoon. Six is used to automobiles. He doesn't realize that they're only good in just certain little narrow strips. It's a different matter, gathering up riders from all over five ranges."

"What do you aim to do? Catch up on your sleep?"

"I'm going to Moloch. I failed when it came to saving Dundee, but maybe I can clear up his name."

"How?"

"By going to Moloch today and picking up the killer. I think I can get help there, now . . . if only I can find out who's my man."

Elmer let out a humorless guffaw. "Just that little if. Good grief, Missouri."

"I'm a darn' sight nearer than you think," said Missouri sharply.

"What do you want me to do?"

"Wait for Holt. I won't need you in Moloch. Elmer, it's pretty needful that Holt know what's going on."

"I'm just as pleased," said Elmer Law, "with this southeaster coming up. There'll be smoke piling down on Moloch until you can't see a foot ahead, and me with a leaning toward asthma and . . ."

"Holy snakes! Southeast it is! Pile out of that car, Elmer! I've got him! I know I've got him!"

"You gone crazy, too?" Elmer stared mournfully after the careening car as it roared its way westward toward the far stacks of Moloch.

At the Moloch jail Sloper found the lank, weary deputy who had first tried to arrest Law and Sloper when they struck Moloch five days before.

"Hardly hoped to find you," said Sloper.

"I don't hold with this posse business," said the deputy. "Nor anything else this Mort Six crowd does, for that matter. I'm just in office as a concession to the cattle crowd."

"I figured that," said Sloper.

"I been pretty helpless," the deputy grunted. "The sheriff's in a tight place, though, now. Mort Six is going to drop from under him, if I read the signs."

"You know Dundee's dead?"

"I heard that, but it wasn't definite."

"It's definite now."

The deputy swore. "And the real killer is alive and free, I'll bet my bottom dollar."

"And in Moloch," said Sloper.

"In Moloch?"

"Want to lay hands on him today?"

The deputy considered him. "I suppose you're another with a hot tip. Well, I've heard a lot of 'em, but none yet that . . ."

Sloper took off his gun belt and laid it on the table beside the deputy's boots. "I'm going to show you that same killer, in the act of trying to gun an unarmed man."

"Who's this is going to be gunned?"

"Me."

"And by who?"

"I don't know."

The deputy grinned wearily.

"Let's try this," Sloper urged him, "if you can bring yourself to walk up the street."

"If I thought I could lay hands on the man that killed Rathbone," said the deputy bitterly, "I'd walk from hell to breakfast on my hands and knees. I worked for Rathbone once."

"Come on, then."

"Cowboy, I'll go with you." The deputy's feet came down with a bang.

"I just want you to walk around the town, a little way behind me."

"And what do I do?"

"You're the trap. I'm the bait."

"And if the bait is snapped?"

"The trap is supposed to close."

"It sounds unlikely to me," the deputy said. "I'll do like you say, though, on the off chance. You act pretty sure."

"Keep me just in sight through the smoke, but if somebody joins me, drop back. And if you hear a shot, or the like . . ."

"That means you're listed for boot hill already, and there's no call to hurry, huh?"

"It means come get your man. I'll be going into some saloons . . . you don't need to follow me into them, hard as it may seem to stay out."

Sloper moved out into the single street of Moloch, and the peculiar acrid yellow smoke swept over him, scouring his throat. Behind him, barely in sight, but no more, moved the indistinct shadow that was the deputy.

"I'll have the killer of Walt Rathbone inside of an hour," Sloper told the bartender in the Gun Rack, "and I'll have him alive."

"The hell you say," was the skeptic answer. "Anybody important?"

Certain things had turned clear in Sloper's mind. "I think," he said, "you'll find his brother is thought important."

"Brother?"

Sloper passed on to the Horse's Neck, to the Palace, to the Last Chance. Moloch had five saloons; Sloper planted his message in them all.

Then, nothing happened, and slowly he walked up and down that single street twice, four times, five, while the smoke settled deeply in his lungs, and within him grew a suspicion that he had failed. It was not the first time, nor the last, and, after all, perhaps it did not matter now to quibble over the name of a man who was dead, and a girl who he might never see again.

Out of the doorway of the Horse's Neck a figure stepped, and Missouri saw that the man was peering into his face through the smoke.

"Hello, Sloper."

"Why, hello, Stam," said Missouri, his voice unwelcome and strange. "Thought I heard that you were killed last night?"

"Slugged in the arm," Stam explained, showing

him a wrist and hand bandaged to the fingertips. "Had to walk back, was all."

"It threw me off, Stam . . . almost. But now it's all pretty plain."

"What's this," said Stam, "about you gunning for the killer of Walt Rathbone? I stuck by Dundee better than a brother, but, between you and me, I swear I've thought all the time that he . . ."

"Like a brother, Stam? That's odd, too. It was just today that I figured out that you probably did have a brother."

"Me . . . a brother? Who told you that?"

"He did . . . or as good as did, Stam."

"*Mmm*. Ain't that kind of funny. Expect we better have a drink on it, huh? Now up here at the Gun Rack they've got . . ."

Smooth, easy, plausible that casual voice. Stam glanced back over his shoulder, and Sloper, following his eye, saw that the deputy was no longer a visible dogging shadow. Lou Stam smiled, that quick-flashing smile that so changed his face, but somehow it looked a good deal harder now than when Missouri had seen it first.

"I guess you know what I mean, Stam," said Sloper, his voice slow and low.

"Well, whatever it is, let's have our drink first." The bandaged left arm slid genially through Sloper's elbow. "Come on."

Then suddenly those treacherous bandaged fingers closed, sharply as jaws, on the wrist of

Missouri Sloper's gun hand. Lou Stam's lips drew back from his teeth like a death's head, and Sloper heard the jerk of steel out of leather, and the hammer's *click*.

With his left hand he clutched at the rising gun, but, although his knuckles struck it, he missed his grip as it blazed, striking like a knife stroke across his left thigh. His left leg gave from under him so that he toppled, but, as he fell forward, he wrenched his right hand free and struck out with all he had. He heard a bone go in his hand at the impact, but felt no pain, and then he was down under the smoke, bearing down the gun hand of the half-conscious man while he waited, waited everlastingly for the arrival of the deputy.

Moloch observed a queer, strained minute of silence, while everyone listened. Then, gradually at first, men began to move again, and to come out of saloons. Through the swirl of the sulphur smoke sounded shouted questions and hurrying feet, and Moloch stirred itself to find out who was killed this time, under the creeping cloud.

Exactly four hours and eighteen minutes later, in Moloch's loopholed adobe jail, Lou Stam confessed to the murder of three men—Rathbone, Laughlin, and Stucky; to the instigation of the mob action that led to the death of Dundee and the wounding of eight Moloch men; to the attempted murder of Missouri Sloper. At that hour, it was known later, two deaths more had already occurred that were to be added, indirectly, to the record of Lou Six, alias Stam, but these were not yet known to anyone in Moloch, and were not covered in the original statement of the accused.

XI

It was a glum gathering to which Missouri Sloper carried the news at the Bar Five that night. Dundee had been buried under the pepper trees that afternoon, but the dozen or so cowboys who had gathered to no purpose, as a result of Art Humphreys's ride to the Box Bar, still lingered, partly, no doubt, to see what they could eat.

Art Humphreys was there, and Al Closson, and Jimmy Rathbone, who Sloper now met for the first time—a young man of twenty or so who for some reason seemed to show all the characteristics of a drink of water, but no others. One man Sloper noticed was Ike Trumbull of the Box Bar, a grizzled veteran of the range with a build like Holt himself.

And Gail Dundee was there, with tubby but good-hearted Mrs. Rathbone. After all, the presence of Gail, and an overly warm sympathy for her bereavement, probably had more to do with the lingering of all those cowboys than did the food. Sloper was amazed, considering what had transpired, when Gail sent him a rather wan smile as he came in. There were dark circles under her eyes, but he noticed at once that she was the center of light in that low dark room, as always wherever he saw her.

Sloper painfully eased his wounded leg and, when the first shock of the news had died sufficiently to let him speak, transmitted to them the principal substance of Lou Stam's confession. Stam now stated that he was the brother of Mort Six, who, incidentally, could not be found. Stam gave no reason for having changed his name, but at least one previous killing was believed to be on his record. Having come to the Tonopah to join his brother two years before, he had found Mort Six in disappointing circumstances—staving off bankruptcy. He had then gone to work for Dundee, principally because he had fallen hard for Gail Dundee.

Lou had expected to find his brother rich, and, as time went on and he made no headway with Gail, his disappointment increased, rather than lessened. He worked hard, to give a good impression, and succeeded to the foremanship of the Bar Five, but it was his belief that he could win Gail if he had money.

Mort Six, by Lou's statement, had always done all he could for his brother, and Lou knew that, if Mort had been a millionaire, Lou would have been sitting pretty enough. When the chance to recoup through the Three Brand lode appeared, Lou determined to stop at nothing to secure for his brother—for purely selfish reasons—the possession of the Three Brand copper. To this end, he had constantly kept an eye on the Three Brand property, hoping against hope that the assessment work would be permitted to lapse. Thus it happened that he was in the hills of Los Muertos on Thursday, June 24th, when Rod Laughlin arrived with his Mexicans to begin the belated assessment work. To try what he then attempted would not have occurred to Stam had he not hated Rod Laughlin because of Rod's standing with Gail. The chance that the Three Brand would not be visited again for a week—by which time the assessment period would be up—was a very slim one. Yet Stam took that long chance. He lay on the rim of Three Brand Gulch and picked Rod Laughlin off with a .303 high-powered rifle.

As Stam expected, the Mexicans under Laughlin made a bolt for the border, knowing very well that they would be the first suspected of the murder. Stam realized that in all likelihood the death of Laughlin would be discovered, and the assessment work would begin in time. The real hope of the brothers, Lou and Mort Six, was that Rathbone would cease wavering and decide to join Dundee in selling out the Three Brand over Holt's head. The $300,000 that Six was offering amounted to nothing compared with the value of the lode. The

Sixes were millionaires—if Rathbone would give in. And Rathbone almost did. On Saturday, June 26th—the day that Rathbone was to die—Stam was riding with Dundee, when they met Rathbone. Dundee and Rathbone took up their argument—to sell or not to sell—where they had last left it off, and this time Dundee apparently succeeded in winning Rathbone over. Dundee sent Stam back and rode with Rathbone to Moloch to close the deal.

Stam, however, eager to learn the outcome, picketed his horse, caught a fresh one, and rode to Moloch by another way. Lou had a prophetic fear that the deal would somehow fall through, and he still had a card in the hole, even if Rathbone refused, and the legal assessment work should be done. Stam had no doubt that Jimmy Rathbone would sell, if ever he inherited control from his father. And Lou had already decided that, if Rathbone refused Mort Six's offer this time, Jimmy was going to inherit—instantly.

By luck, a southeast wind was bearing heavily upon Moloch, so that Lou was readily able to remain unrecognized, and lie low, waiting for the outcome. His horse he left by the water trough—the black horse noticed by Art Humphreys—and walked on toward the smelter through the smoke. But people were moving about the smelter so constantly that he was unable to reach his brother, after the Rathbone interview, without being seen.

He therefore followed Rathbone to the White Front Hotel, where Dundee was waiting, and listened outside the window of Dundee's room. There, eavesdropping, he learned that, as far as Walt Rathbone was concerned, the Sixes had no further hope of purchasing the Three Brand. Stam killed Walt Rathbone in the shrouding smoke that night. In his statement Stam insisted that Rathbone had been first to go for his gun, but this received no credence from anyone.

From Moloch Stam went back to the Bar Five by a back trail leading him near Los Muertos Vivientes, and he turned aside to see how went the other branch of his two-chance hope. Harry Stucky was camped at the mouth of the gulch, evidently mystified by his failure to find life at the mine the night before. Lou Stam, making a circuit, ambushed Stucky—by rifle again—from the rim of the gulch, as Stucky rode up to see what he could find by daylight.

The fact that Rod Laughlin had been dead two days without discovery led Stam to hope that discovery could be held off a few days more. The assessment period closed in three days and a half. He killed Stucky remorselessly to prevent his carrying the news.

The following day—Monday—word reached the Bar Five that Jimmy Rathbone, contrary to expectations, would not join Dundee in selling to Mort Six, but would support Holt's plan for the

Tonopah water. That day Stam, with but one hope left—that the Three Brand title would lapse—returned once more to the hills of Los Muertos, haunting those millions in copper beside which lay the two murdered men. This time Dundee, riding separately, also visited the mine, to check up on Laughlin, and Stam, watching from a distant concealment, perceived that all the risk he had run had come to nothing. And now, from another direction, he saw the three riders from the Cross Hook—Holt, Sloper, and Law—approaching across the plain.

No man ever tried a more forlornly desperate trick than what Lou Stam, in the bitterness of his disappointment, attempted now. At almost the limit of range he put the three Cross Hook men under fire, killing Law's horse. Later, he took a shot at Dundee's horse, also, as opportunity offered, all this in the hope that Dundee and Holt would blame the hostilities on each other and that in the resulting explosion of wrath and scandal all up and down the range the essential assessment work would go forgotten just two days more. That whole plan was a last thin expedient, a forlorn hope. And yet—it appeared to have served its purpose, in the end.

Stam himself admitted that the attempt was hastily conceived, and explained it by saying that it involved little risk, except that his position happened to be near that which Sloper chose.

Stam had expected Sloper to lie low until Stam could get away in the dark. But Sloper got up and almost walked over him, and Stam had been forced to fire upon him at close range, giving away the fact that there was a strange gun in the cañon. Stam denied that he had attempted to kill anyone in this cañon skirmish, and claimed that the creasing of Dundee's leg had been an accident, when he had aimed at the horse.

Then—what Lou had not counted on—rumblings of the wrath of the Tonopah began coming to Moloch. Lou, sent to Moloch by Dundee, found his brother in a state of the utmost apprehension. Mort Six, knowing nothing of what Lou had done, really believed that Dundee had killed Rathbone, but foresaw that the anger of the cattlemen was turning ponderously upon Six himself, due not only to the confusion of the issue but to the dislike in which Mort Six was held in the Tonopah.

Mort Six put the sheriff upon Dundee in good faith. But it was Lou Six, alias Stam, who, knowing Dundee's innocence, decided that Dundee must be sacrificed before he could clear himself of suspicion, thus ending the hunt for the Tonopah killer. It was Lou who gave away Dundee's hide-out at Black Gulch, and conceived the plan of cutting off Dundee's retreat up the gulch and surrounding him with a posse. And it was Lou who had the coolness to hold out fifteen of the best horses in Moloch for the final taking of the Three Brand claim at noon Wednesday, when the previous holders would be automatically disqualified under the law by their own failure to do the assessment work. He foresaw that Holt would raise cowboys to fight for that claim, and that the cattlemen would join to re-stake under new names, so he enlisted, on shares, the toughest men in Moloch to seize the open claim.

It only remained for Lou to make a show of good faith. He rode hard out of Moloch, as he would have done if he had meant to warn Dundee. A few miles from Moloch he stopped and drew blood from his horse by thrusting a stick up its nose, and with this bloodied his saddle and let the horse go back. He then bandaged his arm and returned afoot to Moloch at his leisure. But one thing Lou had not foreseen—that his brother Mort Six, rapacious and hard-dealing though he might be, was essentially upright. When Lou proudly explained to Mort what he had done, Mort hurled himself upon him with his fists, then refused to have anything to do with the matter, declared he would leave the Tonopah, and strongly advised Lou to make a bolt. Lou lay low in the Horse's Neck saloon, a house friendly to Six, half uncertain what to do, now that his brother had failed him. And there the news found him that Sloper knew the truth at last. Thinking himself cornered, Lou decided upon one more killing to save himself, and walked out into the swirling, masking sulphur smoke of Moloch—to his undoing.

When Sloper had finished his story, there was a silence.

"I can't believe it," said Gill Meade of the Two Diamond at last.

"It's true, though," said Sloper.

"How on earth," said Meade, "could any man attempt anything as far-fetched as that play in the gulch, where he shot at Holt, then Dundee, figuring the two to jump each other and forget a million-dollar lode?"

"But, darn it . . . it worked!" said Ike Trumbull. "What with that very thing, and one thing and another, that assessment work *did* go undone. Didn't me and two of my boys ride over there this afternoon, and wasn't we beat off by that very same party of fifteen re-stakers? I tell you, that Lou Stam is too modest . . . it was a good scheme, hasty or not, and well carried out. And it won . . . at least so far as that the Three Brand owners are beat. And except for Sloper here, it seems that Lou Stam would have got away with it."

"What you haven't told us," said Gill Meade to Sloper, "is how you spotted him."

"He gave himself away," said Sloper, "by trying to take me with the deputy right behind me."

"But you must have known?"

"Oh, I had some kind of wild guesses lined up."

181

"And how are we going to get you to tell about that line up of guesses?"

"They sound pretty foolish, but I don't mind. I figured that Rod Laughlin was the first killed, and that there must have been some other motive besides just the long chance of lapsing the title. So I tried to find out who hated Rod. But Rod was liked by everybody, it seemed. It had to be somebody, I thought, that was jealous of him because of Gail . . . and that put Al Closson out, because he didn't pay Gail any attention, though I admit I had suspected Al first of all because of the ridden-out horse he brought in Sunday."

"I always ride a horse pretty hard," said Closson.

"Sure. Then the black horse with the blaze face, by the water trough in Moloch that Saturday night . . . I thought maybe that was mixed up in it. If it was, that told me the man I was looking for was a Bar Five man because, although anybody could pick up a Bar Five horse and ride it, a man with a killing in his mind wouldn't want to be found riding the wrong brand of horse, making it look funny, when he could easy explain having come to town for a drink or something if he had to.

"Then, the mud on the board under Dundee's window . . . I guessed that into the picture, too, because it fitted in with the black horse and the water trough mud, and it suggested that my other guess was right, it being kind of out of the way to listen outside windows. So assuming the listener was the killer, it eliminated Mort Six, who couldn't have anything to learn. Yet Mort Six was the only one who stood to benefit by the killing of Rathbone. I began trying to think of somebody whose interests were pretty well tied up with Mort Six's, and couldn't think of any. And though I suspected Lou Stam when Dundee's hide-out was tipped off, he was reported dead then, and I didn't know what to think.

"But finally, when Mort Six came out to see Holt this morning, I saw how cut up he was, as if he'd found out some pretty hopeless facts, and he made me believe him when he said he wasn't interested in the copper any more. And . . . just then it came to me, Lou Stam and Mort Six look alike. Not much alike. There's a long stretch between a cow foreman and a smelter owner . . . they dress different and everything, and I hadn't noticed any resemblance before. But suddenly I jumped to the conclusion that, if Mort Six had a renegade brother, and that brother was Lou Stam, everything would be clear. And then I was pretty sure that Lou Stam wasn't dead . . . and that, if he wasn't, the thing was simple. Pretty thin . . . just guesses . . . guesses like you make twenty times an hour in trailing out a deer."

"But you got him," said Ike Trumbull. "And I take off my hat."

"I don't see what good it does," said Sloper. "We lost the mine."

Speak for yourself!" said Elmer Law. He was leaning against the side of the open door.

"And where did you come from?" Sloper demanded. "I didn't hear any horse come up."

"I don't feet-step like a horse," Elmer protested wearily, "not at the end of four thousand million miles afoot. But . . . you people ain't lost your mine."

"Haven't lost . . . ," began Jimmy Rathbone.

"It's been bought for you," said Elmer. "Bought for you by a better man than you or me, or any of us, and now that you aren't going to see him any more, I say you're a low breed of folks if you don't see that the Tonopah gets its water, that he's always wanted."

"Elmer, what are you talking about?"

Elmer Law closed the door behind him and leaned against it, and they saw that all the starch and all the sardonic clowning had gone out of him. Of those in the room who had, up to now, given Elmer any thought at all, none had ever thought of him as anything but a young man. But they saw that he did not look young now, but old, and weary, and gray.

"I'm going to tell you, but I want some coffee first."

XII

Jerkily, but with a minimum of words, Elmer Law told his story. Description was not in it, nor any underlining of the meaning of the bare facts he told, but his listeners were able to fill those things in, each according to the quality of his own intelligence and imagination.

Elmer Law had been the only man at the Cross Hook when old Horntoad Holt had ridden home, about the middle of the forenoon, on a slathered and ruined horse. He had hunted Six for two days, but Six had managed to avoid him. Holt was whooping like an Indian, and at first Elmer thought that he was drunk, but this was wrong. Elmer ran out to meet him.

"You the only one here?" Holt demanded.

Elmer told Holt that he was.

"Then saddle!" Holt yelled at him. "Saddle quick!"

Law was already saddled. If he hadn't been, he would have been minutes behind Holt, for the old warrior, having loosed his latigo on the run, brought his saddle off with him as he came to the ground, and had the bridle clear before the pony had come to a stumbling stop. He raced to the corral, threw down the upper two of the four bars, and had a fresh pony saddled before Elmer Law had his loose cinch tightened—almost. Holt jumped his pony over the remaining two bars of the gate and headed northwest toward Los Muertos, riding hard.

A bunch of questions were in Elmer's head, but Holt's hard, leathery face, with its bitter lines and that blue three-cornered scar under one eye was set uglier than ever, and did not seem to invite questions very much. Elmer spoke to the old man just once.

"This horse," he said, "won't ever be rode again, Mister Holt, if we keep on like we been." Elmer was always soft about spoiling a horse.

Holt just nodded, and kept on paying out the horseflesh. He knew what those ponies could do, and he meant to have all they had right now.

It wasn't until they topped the long rise, where you first sight Los Muertos Vivientes, and those dark hills loom up so suddenly at you out of the plain, that Holt told Elmer what it was about.

"Ride closer," he said, and Elmer put his pony over.

"You understand mining law?" Holt asked.

"No," said Elmer.

"You only need to know three things," Holt told him, "to understand what we're going to do now . . . if we ain't too late. The first is . . . you have to do a hundred dollars' assessment work on an unpatented claim every year, in order to hold your rights, but where three claims are held in common by three men, work done on any one of them counts for all. The second thing is . . . if you don't start work, you're disqualified from relocating for three years . . . which is the same as forever, in this case. And the third thing . . . if you start work on the very last day, and pursue it continuously thereafter until the amount is worked out, that claim stays yours, even though the work isn't all done before noon of the last day. I guess you know," Holt finished, "that the Three Brand time is up at noon today. But I don't know whether you know this . . . that fifteen men are on the way to Los Muertos from Moloch, aiming to re-stake the Three Brand claim at noon."

What Elmer didn't see was what two men were going to be able to do about it, and he said so. He had been watching a kind of low-hanging cloud, off to the left behind some low hills; it was a dust cloud, and he was sure by now that the dust had not been stirred up by cattle.

"When I swing down from the saddle," said Holt, "the assessment work starts on the Three Brand. It's the last day and pretty near noon, but it'll hold the claim. And tomorrow you fellers can bring up guards and go on with the work."

A cold perspiration broke out on Elmer's forehead, and his hands turned damp within his buckskin gloves. Law or no law, when fifteen pretty tough customers showed up, all gay with whiskey and the idea that they were rich, and found two lonely men opposing the idea—Elmer knew that a couple of fine points of law were going to be kind of brushed over, right then and there, and that nobody was ever likely to find what was left of those two men, so deep they'd be, down under some rocks.

"So we're going to git in some work," said Elmer, so weakly that his voice was rubbed out by the laboring thrum of the running hoofs beneath, and Holt had to ask him to repeat.

"I didn't say we," Holt pointed out. "I said me. I got other work for you in mind . . . providing we ever reach the diggings at all."

Elmer Law, about then, had a pretty miserable picture of himself, in person, trying to stand off that roused-up mob of Moloch men, while Holt did his work. Elmer jumped to the conclusion that he was elected as mine guard. He was wrong about that, though. Holt had nothing so crazy as that in mind, but something else that did not, after all, involve any particular danger to the person of Elmer Law.

They did reach the diggings, all right. No one was there yet to oppose them. Just before they rode into Three Brand Gulch, Holt drew in his horse and looked back to examine that dust cloud that had been dogging their left, behind the low hills. And they saw now that it was no longer just a dust cloud. A long, trailing straggle of little wiggling dots had come over the crest, and those dots were horsemen that were now about five miles away. First one, then two more, and so on, strung out for a long way, so that you couldn't tell how many were coming who were not yet in sight. Elmer's scalp crawled.

Holt and Law unstrapped their rifles and rode up the gulch at the stumbling jog that was about all the horses had left. You have plenty of room to kill horses, in a nineteen-mile run.

When Holt set foot within the Three Brand monuments, he grinned for the first time. From what happened afterward, it is plain that he knew then, when he stepped down onto that land, that he had won, and that the Three Brand was not going to change hands. But there was a queer sardonic quality in that grin, too, for it is just as certain that he knew what else was ahead.

Holt took a long envelope out of his pocket—it was pretty well folded and crumpled up—and got out a couple of sheets of legal bond, with writing all over them. He signed his name to the bottom of one with an indelible pencil, and had Elmer Law sign underneath as witness.

"I could have used a couple more men," Holt grumbled, "but you'll have to do. This other paper is made out in advance. You're not to use it as it is, but copy it off in your own hand, changing it according to what you see happen here today, then get it into a safe place as quick as you can, and see that the right parties know where it is.

That last," he explained, "is so if you get killed later and can't appear as witness. Now don't lose that, in heaven's name." He gave Elmer the envelope. "Now give me your rifle and six-gun," Holt ordered.

Elmer protested at this, but he did as he was told. "If trouble breaks here . . . and it'll break, as sure as hell burns powder! . . . I'll be helpless as a jay bird, without no guns."

"That's what I want," Holt agreed. "No heroic rescue stuff from you, son. You got to live and bear witness, until this mess is straightened out. I know your breed. Give you so much as a popgun, you'd be right in the thick of it, just itching to die for the dear old brand. Blah! Get this . . . if you get shot, you'll make suckers of us all."

Holt then told him what he was to do. He showed Elmer a ledge, 100 feet up the side of the gulch. It could be reached by a man who climbed with his stomach and his teeth as well as with his hands, and once there it was possible to get up and out over the rim on foot, without showing yourself any more. Elmer was to go up there and watch whatever came off. After that he was to back out quietly, and get to some friendly ranch. That was all.

"How'll I get anywhere without no horse?" Elmer wanted to know, being more or less confused by a train of events he did not, at the time, fully understand.

Holt exploded at him. "What do I care how? Grease your pants and slide. Now git to your post. And damn you, if you come butting in, or so much as show your head . . ."

Elmer obeyed. From his lofty look-out, he watched Holt get a pick and shovel from among the tools that had already been hauled there by Rod Laughlin, and begin to dig—not in the location shaft already begun, but in a new place, so that Law could testify afterward that he saw the old man at work.

In the sharp sunlight the pick rhythmically rose and fell, then presently the shovel, then the pick began.

The first riders of the cavalcade from Moloch were clattering up the gulch. Elmer Law turned his eyes from that rising, falling pick to watch them come. The first to turn the bend of the gulch was one man alone. He jumped his horse to a stop as he sighted Holt 100 yards ahead, and sat there uncertainly for perhaps a minute, while the hoofs of the strung-out horses behind him beat ever stronger and stronger—a ghostly, rising diapason echoing from the unseen.

At that distance, and from above, Elmer Law could not see this man's face. But somehow the hulking loom of the figure on the horse made him think that it was the same bearded giant who had been the first to speak to Missouri and himself in Moloch when they had carried the body of Walt

Rathbone into the Gun Rack Bar—and had so nearly cost them their lives.

Now a second horse, and a third, came clipping it around the bend of the gulch, riders quirting up their horses in the last few rods of the long way from Moloch, and these, too, pulled up beside the first. After that appeared more and more, until almost a dozen were arrayed there in a ragged group that was neither mass nor line.

Yet all this time there continued that slow rise and fall of old Holt's pick. Elmer's scalp began to crawl again. There was something irrational, weird in the way the old man just kept on with his work, as if he did not see or hear those mounted, watching men.

It was bothering the Moloch men, too. They could not make it out. Plainly they suspected a concealed guard, or an ambush. Even Elmer Law, who had good reason to know that he and Holt were alone, was wondering, as he fingered his empty holster, what unheard-of trick old Holt was holding back.

The leaders of the Moloch men appeared to confer, then the gaunt, bearded giant—the one who had ridden first—dropped from his horse and walked toward Holt.

Holt had not seemed to see, or hear, but his eyes must have been upon that man all the time, for as the tall hard-rock man stepped past the monument that marked the beginning of the Three Brand, Holt dropped his pick.

The horses of those laggards last to arrive still made an incessant ruffle of sound that reëchoed in the lower cañon, but everybody there heard the big voice of Horntoad Holt as he roared out his challenge.

"I warn you off this claim!"

The tall man hesitated, then hunched his shoulders obstinately and came on. "Oh . . . you do?"

"I warn you," said the powerful voice of Holt again, "that I stand on my rights, as a co-owner of this claim. Get off, or by the Almighty, I'll gun you down!"

"Listen, you," said the trespasser. "I don't want any trouble with you. Your assessment work ain't done . . . your title to the claim runs out within the hour. We got a right here, and damned if we won't fight for our rights."

"The assessment work is begun, right here with this here pick," Holt answered. "You know the law as good as I. Off, now, or take your poison."

Once more the giant hesitated. No doubt he still feared ambush, or some hidden strategy behind the old man's defiance of overwhelming odds. But behind him he heard the growl of those mounted men, and as a leader he dared not cheapen himself in their eyes. He once more moved toward Holt.

"Take it, then!" roared Holt, and his twin guns came flashing up in his two hands.

The gaunt miner flinched and braced himself as if he had suddenly been struck by a mighty wind, then his own gun came up and smashed out once, without effect. Holt's two guns spoke almost together. The tall, bearded man started, doubled up with both arms across his stomach, and took two queer, stiff steps forward before he slumped inertly to the ground to move no more.

Holt holstered his guns, and there was a certain finality in the movement of his hands as he slapped the weapons back into their worn leather, as if their work was done for all time. Then, deliberately, he stooped and picked up his pick, and there he faced the men of Moloch, feet wide, the pick in his two hands across his thighs—a tall, lonely figure, with the sunlight behind.

From the disorderly ranks of the horsemen came a snarling growl, and the skittering sound of nervously shifting hoofs. A .45 crashed, then two more together, and still Gideon Holt stood motionless, his pick in his hands. Then the subtly variant voice of a rifle spoke, and Holt jerked, seemed to stiffen—and pitched face forward into the shallow hole he himself had dug.

"And then," Elmer Law put it. "I come away."

There was a silence, heavy and inert, until Ike Trumbull broke it gently.

"The last of the three," he said. "Rathbone . . .

Dundee . . . Holt. Friendly ranchers, once, and . . . they're dead . . . and hating each other, every one of them. That copper was awful bad medicine for them."

"I see there's a note in this envelope he give me," Elmer Law added. "It's for you, Missouri."

Missouri took the scribbled slip of paper Elmer Law handed him and read:

> Missouri:
> This here document evidence is yours. Fire fights fire. For God's sake, use your head and don't let this business get bungled up in no court of law.
> G. Holt.

Behind the scribbled words Missouri was conscious of other words—words he had heard spoken by Gideon Holt: *An old man has a right to spend himself, like a bullet out of a gun.*

"The other things in this envelope," Elmer was saying, "are just his affidavit that he is starting assessment work at such and such an hour and date, with me as witness, and a kind of outline affidavit showing how he wants me to write out my testimony of what I seen . . . how he was doing the work when interrupted by force."

There was a long silence, a silence of shock, of incomprehension.

"Do you think we can go to law with those

papers?" Jimmy Rathbone began doubtfully. "What does he mean? Did he suppose we could take a couple of affidavits and . . . ?

"It can't be done," said Trumbull with finality. "They'd have twenty witnesses to your one. If that's all the Three Brand case boils down to, it ain't worth the powder to blow it up."

"Good grief," Jimmy Rathbone cried out, "he must have known that gang would . . . !"

"You bet he knew," said Elmer Law.

"Then . . . he's thrown away his life for just nothing!" Gail cried.

"He has not," said Sloper. "Can't you see? This whole thing is based on his opinion of what he called the average man. A kid can stand off the average mob with a candy stick, he once told me, and he's left us with a saddle whack of dynamite. I tell you, we'll have justice yet.

"By this time the Three Brand is re-staked . . . by nobody but the pack that were in on the death of Holt. Under the law they are all equally guilty. Some of that bunch will have to go back to Moloch for supplies . . . and when they do . . . there's a deputy in Moloch that will play our game . . . nor will the sheriff stop him, either. We'll find out who those men are easy enough, and slap all we lay hands on into the coop. Then out with the third degree, and, if half don't turn state's evidence, then Holt was wrong. But even if they don't . . . let one of them get away and go back to the rest . . . *after* he's seen these affidavits as to what happened at the Three Brand. Let him think we've got plenty more. Three days from now you can look for that bunch of claim-jumpers in Mexico. As soon as one of 'em bolts, they'll scatter and blow for cover like quail, and the country won't hold their hot riding."

"They'll jump like the guilty flea you've heard about," said Elmer.

"They know by now that Lou Stam is out from under them . . . and Mort Six, too," Sloper went on. "Trumbull, take this bunch of cowboys and gather them . . . half a dozen at a time . . . within sight of Los Muertos Camp just out of range. You can have a mighty anxious bunch of claim-jumpers within twelve hours, and in three days . . ."

"They'll slip through our fingers, sure," said Trumbull pessimistically.

"And isn't that what you want? Let them slide across the border. Holt wanted to save the Three Brand. I say he has."

"You know," said Trumbull slowly, "I think Holt picked him the right man. This is going to work."

"By heaven, it's got to work," said Sloper.

Within the week, it did.

XIII

It was at the end of that week that Sloper next saw Gail Dundee. He rode to see her at the Crazy K, where she was still staying.

"I'll thank you to hold my horse, Elmer," said Missouri. "I'll tell Miss Dundee good bye for you."

Elmer nodded. Missouri had expected the usual argument, but there was none.

"I'll be going now, Miss Dundee," he told her when he stood hat in hand before her in the big living room.

"You'll be what?"

"I'm leaving the Tonopah now. What little I can do is done. Three Brand men are at work on the mine in the gulch, and the last of the claim-jumpers is over the border, barring the two wounded, who are in jail waiting for the grand jury along with Lou Stam. The Three Brand has had a close call, Miss Dundee . . . the whole thing would have been just the other way around in another day. But it's over, thanks to Gideon Holt."

"And to you," said Gail.

"No, I played no part, Miss Dundee."

"I'll argue that another time. Didn't you get my message, saying I wanted to see you?"

"Yes, but I was busy, and I knew I'd be coming in a day or two anyway, to say good bye."

"But you can't go, Missouri . . . the whole range is already posted that you're the new manager for the Bar Five."

"I'm not such a good foreman, Miss Dundee, and I . . ."

"There's a whole lot more than a foreman's work at the Bar Five now, with all those mining arrangements, and the deals to make for the dam, and organizing to split the water benefits to everyone in the Tonopah . . . there's three other brands to be counted in, you know, and better stock for the range . . . a thousand things that I'm so eager to get at, and you have to . . ."

"You don't want me working for you, Miss Dundee."

"For me? With me, then. . . ."

"Not when you stop to think what I told you up Los Muertos . . . and that it was true, every word. I guess you were forgetting that."

Gail shook her head. "No. I wasn't forgetting. That's the reason, more like. Are you so determined to be a saddle bum all your life?"

"Seem like that's what I'm cut out for, Miss Dundee."

"And you're set on leaving the Tonopah?"

"I . . . I'm afraid . . ."

"And you still think you're so good at whatever you try to do, and so set in your own ways . . ." Her voice had suddenly become unsteady.

"No," said Missouri slowly, "I was wrong, and

I've always been wrong . . . and useless. And I know that I've failed you . . . failed you in every way."

"And you're failing me now!" she cried out suddenly, the tears springing to wet eyes.

"Why Gail! Why, Gail . . ."

Suddenly he caught her in his arms, as she turned away.

One Charge of Powder

Everything—life itself, probably—depended upon Shad's conserving that one shot he had left. Just a few moments ago the affair had been merely a hold-up in a lonely mountain cabin, but old Shad Blackhook, with one of his characteristic, unreasoning bursts of temper, had turned it into a murderous siege. His huge voice had boomed out like a thunderbolt as he snatched from the wall that ancient, incredible buffalo gun.

"Now up! And out! Jump, you, before I let you have it!"

The man called Crutcher could still have dropped old Shad from the doorway. But his partner, that fox-sharp, squirrel-quick, little man who called himself George Culp, dropped the tin box he was carrying and leaped for the door like a spring released. Culp's flight knocked Crutcher endways; his automatic exploded into the air, and the two sprawled in the dust outside the door.

Then the heavy door slammed, the bar fell, and from within old Shad Blackhook was roaring: "Now *git!* And I'll drop the last to cross that crick!"

All his life Shad's explosive anger had got him into trouble. He could have been a mine owner or a cattle boss, for he was shrewd, tireless, and thrifty, but always that red berserk fury of his came to the surface in time to frustrate him. Just this once, though, that temper had saved—for the moment, at least—all Shad Blackhook possessed.

Culp and Crutcher had planned their coup carefully, and executed it smoothly. Evidently they had got hold of some pretty detailed information about Shad. They had got in under the pretext of begging breakfast. With a superlatively smooth technique they had first filched Shad's weapons, even down to the last loose cartridge. Then, coolly, they had held him up, and they had known exactly where to find the tin box that contained all the old man had.

Only that aged buffalo gun, pegged high in the shadows under the eaves, had escaped Culp's eye at the last; and this—together with Shad's temper—had spoiled an otherwise perfect job.

Barricaded now within the cabin, old Shad picked a set of loopholes in the mud chinking of the walls, and, when these were done, he kneeled, and began putting spilled yellowbacks and gold pieces back into the tin box that Culp had dropped. His big gnarled fingers were almost tender as they laid the money away. Lately he had counted it pretty carefully and found that he had far more than he had supposed. Enough to keep him comfortable through his remaining years, if only . . .

Suddenly the coins dropped from his fingers,

and he turned to rummaging feverishly among his traps. A cold sweat appeared on his forehead; his powder horn was nowhere to be found. Bullets and caps for the ancient gun he had in plenty, but powder . . . fearfully he examined the gun itself. As he remembered, it still contained one good solid charge. One charge of powder and two well-armed men outside . . .

Presently, when he detected Culp and Crutcher cautiously creeping back, he knew that they must know this, too—that he had but one shot left.

It soon appeared that the besiegers knew even more: they knew that Shad's great weakness lay in his ungovernable temper. From outside, startlingly close at hand, came the voice of George Culp— a leering voice, bold and insolent: "Hey, you, grandpaw . . ." There followed a slow, taunting string of profane insults, reaching Shad distinctly behind the logs.

Old Blackhook's face darkened, and the veins began to stand out on his forehead. The muzzle of the long gun in his hands quivered as he peered out through one of the gun loops he had made. He got hold of himself, however, and slowly let the gun sag. If he wasted that one shot, how long would it take them to crash the door and swarm in upon him with their automatics? He wiped the sweat from his forehead.

Again came George Culp's evil, taunting voice. It was recalling forgotten incidents now, raffishly probing sore spots in Shad's career. Against the inner wall the old man stiffened. His eyes seemed to start from his head, and, although their surface was glazed, there burned within them a terrible light.

Outside the sneering, penetrating voice spoke once more. With the growling whimper of a struck bear, Shad whirled upon the loophole, and the long gun whipped up. He thought he saw the outline of a hat. In a sane moment he would have known that hat was offered him on a stick, bait for the one shot he had left, but now—the hammer of the long gun clicked back . . .

Dusk, the quick sharp dusk of the Lomas de Dios, where night seems to flow into the forested gorges like water, had come. Shad, still listening intently, heard the voices of his tormentors once more. But now they were lowered, and Shad recognized that they were no longer taunting, but weary, exasperated, unnerved.

"It's dark enough," Crutcher was insisting. "Stand up and smash in that door. I'll do the rest."

"Stand up yourself," Culp suggested furiously.

"I will, by God!" said Crutcher.

Softly Shad unbarred the door. Instantly a chunk of rock crashed against it, flinging it wide. Shad snatched up a coat, and cautiously showed it at the side of the doorway, and outside a gun spoke rapidly, almost hysterically, four times.

Shad dropped the coat, and with one hand thrust out his gun, so that the dual barrel showed dimly in the last light.

"Drop him! Drop him!" Culp gibbered. "He's coming out!"

Shad heard the frantic, empty *snap* of an automatic lock. "Drop him yourself!" Crutcher snarled.

"Now, you two!" said Shad, stepping out into the open. "Up your hands. And if one of you makes a break . . . !"

There was a long moment while Crutcher and Culp, each waiting for the other to fire, arrived at the realization that neither of them was able. Their hands went up.

"All right, we're beat," said Crutcher in a dead voice.

Shad stood the pair of faces to the wall, disarmed them, and bound their wrists with heavy string.

"I thought you had plenty of cartridges," Culp snarled at Crutcher. "You would've had plenty, if you hadn't blew up and wasted 'em, trying to shoot through cracks!"

"Who, me? If you hadn't've got sore because you couldn't get him sore, you wouldn't have shot wild the last four. . . ."

"Oh, was you trying to get me sore?" said Shad.

"I can't understand it," Culp kept saying over and over. "Blackhook, you look like a guy that would blow up, and you talk like it, and you got the name of being dynamite, and we knew you had only one charge of powder. But we worked on you all day and tried everything, and damned if I could get you mad enough to let go with it."

Shad chuckled. "I'll tell you the truth," he decided. "You got me mad, all right. But it seems that gun has been resting under a leak in the roof, and I guess the powder was wet. If I snapped that hammer once, I bet I snapped it ten thousand times . . . *but the fool gun wouldn't shoot.*"

Blood Moon

A vague feeling of uneasiness came over Lew Winborn, professional gambler and gunman, as he approached the small, unpainted cabin and corral of the little Waffle Iron spread that he and Larry Stevens owned together. It was a feeling of portending evil.

Naturally superstitious, as most gamblers, believing in hunches and good luck signs, Lew remembered the full moon that had risen, red and large, the previous night. A blood moon, old-timers called it, and they told grim tales of Indian raids in the pioneer days that were foretold by the full moon when it pushed its way upward, red and hideous, in the smoky eastern sky.

Lew had seen it the night when Vincent Hall went down, spitting blood from a punctured lung, and Lew himself had taken two bullets in his powerful body before his blazing .44 ended the career of Snake Gardener and the two hired killers who backed his play.

He had seen it again the night that he won $15,000 from Bliss Quillen, owner of the Rafter J, and his foreman, Mex Lober. Lew would have died that night had not young Larry Stevens horned in, shot the gun out of the foreman's hand, and stood Bliss against the wall till the gambler recovered from the cowardly blow that had been dealt him from behind.

Ironically enough, that $15,000 had gone to pay Larry's debt to the bank and stocked the little Waffle Iron. Out of that night had come the arrangement whereby Lew and Larry became partners and the boy escaped from the clutches of Bliss Quillen who was trying to add the Waffle Iron, with its sections of lush, sub-irrigated hay land, to the Rafter J.

It was thus that Lew gained the eternal enmity of Bliss Quillen, who swore that the gambler's life should pay for that night's work. It was no idle threat, and on account of it Lew sat out of the direct line of fire from the windows when he played poker, and he carefully watched the trail wherever he went. Death, mysterious and sudden, was no stranger to this land where the Rafter J was the law and Bliss Quillen ruled with iron hand.

Riding like a centaur, Lew swayed to the gait of his splendid black gelding. A narrow-brimmed Stetson of dove gray was the only concession he had made to the trail. His black frock coat bulged slightly under the left shoulder, for the profession of Lew Winborn required that a weapon of sufficient size and caliber be concealed in some mysterious place about his person.

His fancy vest was crossed with a heavy gold chain and seals. The tops of his hand-tooled

Mexican boots were worn inside the striped trousers, and on the third finger of his immaculate white hand flashed a diamond of imposing size. His black mustache was carefully groomed, and heavy, black sideburns grew low upon his cheeks, a fitting background for the large, dark eyes that had so often looked upon flaming death in Western gambling hells.

As he rode over a tiny rise, he caught a glimpse of the rider of a snow-white horse disappearing into the narrow defile in the hills that led to Comanche Pass, the only known way over the badlands, where miles of shifting sands and jagged, saw-toothed red rocks spread out in an endless desolation.

Lew frowned slightly as the man drew into the defile, for he had heard ugly tales of a certain rider on a white horse since coming to Rushton a year ago. They were tales of sudden appearances of a masked man on ghostly steed, of the stagecoach held up and the Rafter J payroll taken, of haystacks burned, and small herds of cattle driven away.

There was no sign of life as he approached the ranch. He rode around the corner of the cabin, and then reined the tall gelding up short. For a long moment he sat staring at the object on the ground before him. It was a man, white and still, and a dark red stain was still spreading slowly over the front of his shirt.

With a hoarse cry Lew sprang from the back of his horse and knelt by the fallen man.

"Larry, Larry," he murmured.

He placed his hand over the boy's heart, then withdrew it slowly and remained staring at the white face.

It was a long time before he rose to his feet. Lifting the body of his young partner, he carried it into the cabin, laid it gently on the bed, and covered it with a blanket.

There was a clatter of hoofs and the sound of voices. With grim, set lips Lew stepped out into the sunlight.

"Hyah, Lew?" greeted a tall, burly man with a bushy gray mustache. A silver star gleamed conspicuously on the front of his cowhide vest. At his side rode the ornate Bliss Quillen in silk shirt of sky blue and yellow leather vest bright with studded silver and fancy stitching. His soft doe-skin chaps contrasted oddly with the hair pants of the others.

"Howdy, Sheriff." It seemed to Lew that his voice was strange and far away so great was the emotion tearing at his heart.

Otherwise, he might have spoken ironically of the company the sheriff was keeping. He knew it was not unusual for the sheriff to be riding the range with the man who elected him. Quillen stared closely at the gambler and said nothing.

"We're trailin' this here outlaw that's hidin' out

somewhere in the badlands," explained the sheriff as he swept off his big Stetson and mopped his brow with a red bandanna. "Bliss lost forty-odd four-year-old steers last night, and that nester over on the branch had three stacks of hay burned up this mornin'."

"Yeah," murmured Lew. "He's been here. Larry is dead . . . shot."

With an exclamation the big sheriff swung down from his horse.

A moment later the little group stood over the body of Lew's young partner.

"I'm takin' the trail, Sheriff," Lew stated grimly, "and I will never give it up until I bring him back to be hanged."

"Have you got any idea where to look, Winborn?" asked Quillen.

"Yeah, I think I have. A month ago I was comin' over Comanche Pass in the badlands and I saw smoke a mile or more off to the right jest this side of the red rocks. It's a hunch, mebbe, but I am goin' to find out who is makin' that smoke."

"It's twenty mile at least," declared the sheriff, "an' I can't make it today. In the morning I'll take a few of the boys and go with you."

Lew turned to the tall, rangy gelding and slowly swung to the saddle. His lips were still set grimly.

"I'm playin' a lone hand, Sheriff." Lew gathered up the reins in his gloved hand and the gelding started forward at a touch of his heel. "When you see me comin', I'll be draggin' in this *hombre* by the neck."

"Jest a moment, Winborn!"

Lew pulled up the gelding and looked into the steel-gray eyes of Bliss Quillen. He never had liked those eyes. It seemed to Lew they should shift away from his gaze, but instead they bored steadily into his. They were unwinking, merciless eyes, the eyes of a man who had not the slightest compassion in his heart.

"Well?"

Bliss regarded the gambler a moment. "You'll be wantin' to sell this place," he remarked calmly, "and I want the first chance."

"Listen, Bliss Quillen." Lew's voice was low and even and gave no hint of the rage that was seething within him. "Where I come from it is customary to wait till after the funeral before dividin' up a man's property. You've been after this little spread a long time. You didn't give a hoot how you got it, but I'm tellin' you right here you will never get one part of this land or one critter that's on it. You're dealing with me now, and not Larry Stevens. The boy's grave will be here and I'm not turnin' it over to any dirty range hog."

For a long moment the two men glared at each other.

"I'll remember this, Winborn." Quillen turned away, muttering to himself.

As he rode toward the trail leading into the badlands, Lew noticed a charred and blackened ruin a short distance to the left of the trail. It was all that remained of what had once been the buildings of a small ranch.

Lew had heard the tale of the persecution of the nesters and small ranchers who had been driven out of the country before he came. He knew that this particular spread had been homesteaded by Rance Mainton, a young fellow who had maintained the unequal struggle with strong men who rode only at night, until his buildings had been burned and his cattle scattered.

Bill Dellinger, the sheriff, had discovered the tragedy, but failed to find any trace of the body of young Mainton.

Lew had heard Larry Stevens mention the unsolved crime with tears in his eyes, for he and Rance Mainton had been saddle mates and fast friends.

It was early afternoon. Lew lay behind a soap weed, peering carefully over the red rimrock into a tiny hollow. A clear, cold spring came out in the rock, spread out in a shallow stream, tumbled its way across the little valley, and disappeared among the rocks as mysteriously as it had come.

A few willows had taken root along the stream, and the tiny valley was like a green jewel with the grass that had sprung up and flourished. Standing in the shade of a willow was a man rubbing down a snow-white horse. Saddle and bridle were lying on the grass beside him.

Beneath the cold, stoical exterior of Lew Winborn was a strange gentleness and love for all beautiful things. He drew in his breath sharply as the white horse shoved its nose playfully against its master and saw the affectionate care the man was taking of this beautiful animal. There must be some good, Lew thought, in any man who could love a horse. Then, setting his lips in grim determination, he began making his way down the steep side of the hill, taking advantage of every rock, pausing, creeping quickly forward, leaping, stooping, slipping in and out along the boulders and soap weeds that covered the slope.

Silently, swiftly he made his way forward. The man's back was toward him and he did not turn as Lew approached.

A cold, merciless rage surged over Lew as he crept forward. The still form of Larry Stevens, lying motionlessly on the ground, came before him. This man must die. He must die beneath the limb of a tree, with a rope around his neck. It was the stern, relentless law of the West.

As though prompted by some mysterious sense the man turned. For a moment he stared with wide eyes as Lew rose to his feet a scant twenty yards away. He had taken off his belt and gun and it lay looped over the saddle horn.

"Put 'em high up, you skunk." A Colt .45 appeared in Lew's steady hand.

The gambler's voice was harsh and strained as he barked the order.

Slowly, deliberately the man raised his hands. For the first time Lew noticed that he was a very young man, and the small mustache and flaxen beard could not hide the smooth contour of his cheeks.

"What do you want?" he asked sharply.

"I want you."

With his dark eyes boring into the blue ones before him, Lew strode forward.

"Turn 'round!" he ordered as he drew a thin rawhide thong from his pocket. "Put down your hands and cross them behind you."

Slowly the uplifted hands came down, and then, with a swift movement, the outlaw struck the gun to one side.

The roar of the weapon shattered the stillness, and then a fist caught Lew fairly on the point of the chin. Quick as he was, that lightning movement had caught him off guard. As his head snapped back, his wrist was caught in a vise-like grip, and he dropped the gun in an effort to regain his balance.

Surging forward, he smashed his clenched fist into the face before him. Releasing his grip, the outlaw staggered backward, and the two men stood glaring at each other. A tiny trickle of blood ran down the outlaw's cheek where it had encountered the diamond on Lew's finger.

Then springing forward like a tiger, he struck at this man who had trapped him. Again Lew's head snapped back at the impact of that lightning fist. Springing backward and forward, his feet dancing lightly on the carpet of grass, the bandit drove home blow after blow. Again and again Lew rushed forward, striking out at the smaller youth.

A quick blow to the gambler's nose brought the claret in a steady stream that ran down over the immaculate shirt front and fancy vest.

Lew suddenly realized he had met his match in this slender youth who moved like chain lightning and struck with the power of a trip-hammer.

One—two! One—two! Again and again the young bandit bored in, struck home, and danced away. Lew was reeling and a faint haze seemed to gather about him. Dimly be saw the moving face before him, the eyes, the short flaxen beard, and the thin stream of blood as it trickled down the smooth cheek.

He knew he was fighting a losing battle, yet, gambler that he was, ready at all times to take a chance with money or with life, he was ready to have it out this way.

Time after time he rushed forward, but, like a dancing wraith, the outlaw eluded him, vanishing into the gray mist that seemed to Lew to be settling down into the little valley, springing into view again, with his lightning fists driving home against the red face and weakening body before him.

Clenching his teeth in impotent rage, Lew sought to evade those quick, dancing rushes and the deft blows that were rained upon him. He shook his head in an effort to clear the gray mist that was slowly enveloping him. Struggling with weakness, he sprang forward in a last desperate effort.

Dimly he saw the outlaw go down, and then he himself tripped over a saddle and fell upon the prostrate form. The mist cleared as he fell. With an effort he grasped the outlaw's throat in both hands.

Again and again the lightning fists smashed into Lew's face, but he held on like grim death, exulting in his heart as he realized that the battle was his. The slight body twisted and turned beneath his own. The mouth opened, the eyes rolled back, and then, as suddenly as it had begun, the fight was over. Lew released his grasp upon the outlaw's throat, and watched the deep purple fade into red and white as his prisoner gasped for breath.

Swiftly he cut the latigos from the saddle and in a moment had bound the young outlaw.

"You're shore a devil in a fight, young feller," he remarked evenly through his puffed lips, "but all the same I'm taking you back to hang."

• • •

It was late twilight as they came out of the badlands into the narrow cañon that twisted a tortuous way to the plains. The green of the jack pine and scrub oak was a welcome relief from the shifting sands and red rocks of the badlands. A few feet ahead of Lew rode the outlaw, silent, stoical, forking gracefully the beautiful, snow-white horse, his hands lashed to the saddle horn.

Not a word had passed between the two men since Lew's voice had rung out: "I'm taking you back to hang."

The gambler had washed most of the marks of the struggle from his face, but the lacerated eyebrow, the swollen nose, the bruised cheek, and puffed lips showed the terrific beating he had taken.

As the two horses made their way carefully down the narrow path, a full moon pushed its way upward in the smoky east. It was a hideous moon, red and distorted in the refracted light. A blood moon.

On such a night had the painted, howling horde of savages descended upon the settlements and wagon trains, plundering, burning, killing, to return in the early dawn to their villages drunk with victory and waving trophies of bloody scalps.

What could be the portent of a blood moon this night? Last night it had foretold the murder of

Larry Stevens. Looking at the gracefully swaying shoulders of the man before him, Lew knew the answer. Tonight the murderer of Larry Stevens would hang by the neck until he was dead.

Lew felt a sudden pity for the man before him. Why should one so young, so full of life and strength, choose the way of the outlaw that inevitably must end with flaming guns or a rope thrown over a cottonwood limb? Then the gambler set his lips in a stern line as he remembered the white, still face of Larry Stevens.

They came out upon a wide, open space in the cañon, strewn with huge boulders that stood out, sharp and black, in the red light from the moon. A crash of firearms broke the stillness of the night and vicious stabs of flame from behind four of the boulders.

The white horse reared high with a shrill scream and fell squarely across the path. Lew felt a blow as though someone had struck him in the left shoulder. The ground seemed to rise up and meet him. He knew he had fallen from his horse but he had no recollection of the actual falling. He knew he was badly hit.

Half conscious, he closed his eyes and then opened them as he heard a voice. The great orb of the moon seemed to move about between the high cañon walls, and into the gambler's consciousness came the thought that this was the red moon— the blood moon—that last night had foretold the death of Larry Stevens, and tonight was fore-telling the death of Lew Winborn.

Then things stopped whirling and conscious-ness slowly returned.

Again he heard the voice: "We got 'em both. Come on!"

"Wait! That tinhorn gambler is a hellion in a fight. Wait till you see if they move."

Lew recognized the voice of Bliss Quillen.

He heard the sound of boots coming toward him over the rocks. Feeling weak and sick, he tried to rise, and then fell back again panting with the exertion. Shoving his right hand beneath his coat, he drew the .44 that he carried in a shoulder holster at his left side. The handle of the gun was wet and warm, and there was blood on his right hand that showed black in the moonlight.

A row of small boulders, not more than a foot in height, were between him and the ambushers.

A head came into view above the skyline. The sharp bark of Lew's .44 split the stillness and the head disappeared. Weak and trembling as he was, Lew had fired without taking aim and without thought of hitting the man who approached. His movement was entirely strategic. He had fired to frighten and not to kill.

Again came the sound of voices.

"Did he get you, Mex?" came the voice of Bliss Quillen.

"No! But I sure heard the whistle of the bullet.

The jasper ain't dead, and we've got to get him."

With a supreme effort Lew rolled to his right side. A few feet away lay the white horse, motionless and still. The outlaw had thrown himself out of the saddle as the animal fell and was now lying prone with his hands lashed to the saddle horn. Lew could see his fingers moving as he sought to free himself.

From down the cañon came the low sound of voices. Then, clear and sharp, came the command: "Mex, you and Dave go back and work your way up to the rimrock. Then you can kill 'em like rats in a trap."

Lew knew that he was doomed. There was no shelter he could reach that would protect him from these men once they reached the rimrock.

Near him stood the well-trained black gelding that had not moved since its master had fallen from the saddle. In the moonlight he could see the outlaw's belt and gun hanging from the saddle horn. Again came that feeling of pity for this young man. It was hell for a man to die that way —lying helplessly in plain view to be shot without mercy. It was better for even one who had lived as this outlaw had lived to die standing up, fighting, with his gun in his hand.

Lew's shoulder was throbbing now with a burning pain as though a hot iron had seared his flesh. Stifling a groan, he inched his way toward the fallen outlaw. No word was whispered as he reached the man's side. With an effort he drew a thin knife from one of the mysterious places in the long coat. A quick movement and he had severed the thongs that bound the outlaw's hands to the saddle horn.

As the man regarded him with cold, emotionless eyes, Lew gestured toward his own saddle where hung the holstered gun and the belt bristling with cartridges.

The young man nodded and crawled toward the horse. In a moment Lew saw him rise to his feet on the other side of the black gelding. He saw the gun belt disappear as it was taken from the saddle horn.

He wondered if the two men still in the cañon had seen what was going on. Evidently not, or they would have killed the horse, and then the man. There was no mercy in the heart of Bliss Quillen.

Lew hoped that Quillen would not kill the gelding. After all, there was no object in doing so for there was not the slightest chance of either him or the outlaw escaping on the horse. He saw the outlaw sink to his knees again, and then go running rapidly on all fours along the path they had come.

Yellow! Yellow and running away from the fight. Yet Lew knew the young man was not yellow. After all, why should he stay for the fight? It was Lew's fight and not his.

The realization came to the gambler that this man was escaping, this man who had killed Larry Stevens and for whose capture Lew had come alone into the badlands only to forfeit his life to Bliss Quillen.

With steady hands Lew raised his deadly .44. The young outlaw's body grew large over the sights.

Then his gun dropped. Somehow Lew could not bring himself to kill even the murderer of Larry Stevens in cold blood.

From down the cañon came the crack of a gun followed by the vicious hum of a bullet. The bandit sprang to his feet and dashed up the narrow trail, dodging, stooping, turning, twisting, slipping as the two men in ambush fired again and again at his moving figure.

Lew hoped he would get away, and then wondered why. Why should his sympathy be with the man who killed his friend? Then he knew it was because he had done what Larry Stevens would have done. Larry, soft and tender as a woman, never could have shot a retreating man in the back.

The outlaw disappeared around a jutting side of the cañon and the roar of firearms ceased.

Again he heard the voice of Bliss Quillen: "Let him go. We don't give a hang about him anyway. What we want is this tinhorn gambler and the Waffle Iron."

In the moonlight, Lew could see Mex and the other man climbing toward the rimrock far down the cañon. It would not be long now. He looked about him, but there was no shelter near that would avail against a man above him with a gun. Death would be his portion.

Grimly he smiled, for Lew Winborn was not afraid of death. Often had he looked upon it in all its ugliness amidst the crashing of guns and the curses of dying men. Death! Let it come. Larry would be waiting. In a few moments Lew would join him and together they would go on the great adventure. Lew was glad he had left the young outlaw to be a scourge upon this land.

He watched the two men as they crept slowly upward. Presently they reached the rimrock and disappeared over it. Again Lew looked about him. Slightly more than thirty feet away was a boulder four or five feet high that cast a heavy shadow. Perhaps if he could reach that rock . . .

With a set jaw he struggled to his knees and crawled toward it. Sweat stood out upon his forehead. Then a mist seemed sweeping about him and he sank down, coughing. There was a warm, salty taste in his mouth. He knew the bullet had touched a lung, and that he was tasting blood.

For a long time he lay still, and then trained his gun against the rimrock that stood out sharply against the skyline. At least he would die as he had lived—gun in hand.

The black silhouette of a head appeared and Lew took careful aim. Somehow that head would not remain still but kept moving sideways and jogging up and down. He pulled the trigger. The sharp crack of the .44 echoed up and down the cañon, and the head dodged back.

From above came the sharp roar of a gun. A man sprang into view, whirled completely around, staggered a moment on the rimrock, and then came crashing down into the cañon. As he lay in a pathetic, twisted heap, Lew recognized the dark face of Mex Lober.

The crashing of firearms again sounded from above. From below came the shouting of Bliss Quillen and the other man.

Lew wondered what had happened to Mex Lober, and who was waging that fight on the rimrock. In all Lew's life no one had ever come to his aid except Larry Stevens.

The firing ceased as suddenly as it had begun.

A head and shoulders appeared against the skyline, and again Lew raised his gun. The sights drew into alignment against the rimrock, yet something seemed to hold his hand.

There was a sharp stab of flame as the man fired downward, and the roar of the gun was echoed by a cry of pain from one of the men in the valley. Again and again came that flash of fire from above.

Lew tried to struggle again to his knees, but

he coughed and fell backward. His shoulder throbbed with dull pain and he suddenly realized that the earth was growing very dark and still.

He was aroused by a dash of cold water in his face and a soft voice was speaking to him.

"I'll have that hurt tied up in no time, old-timer," it said. "Then we'll ride double till we reach a ranch."

Lew looked up into the face of the young outlaw.

"You . . . you . . . ," he began.

"Sure! Did you think I'd run out on you? It was Quillen and Lober and that crook, Dellinger, and one of their cut-throats. For more than a year I've been dreamin' about this night. They're dead . . . all four of 'em, and the people in this country can breathe again."

Suddenly to Lew came a great light of understanding.

"Who . . . who are you?" he asked, but he knew the answer before it was given.

"I'm Rance Mainton. Quillen burned me out and thought I was dead, but I fooled 'em. Playin' a lone hand, I've robbed his payroll, burned his hay, an' driven off his steers. With Quillen dead, I'm square with the world and will start my little ranch again."

"But why did you kill Larry Stevens?" Lew asked weakly.

"I didn't. He was my best friend. I reached him just before he died, and he gave me this note for his partner. I don't know who you are, stranger, but I'm beginnin' to suspect we're goin' to get along well together."

He held up a page from a small notebook and Lew read the coarse handwriting:

Lew:
   Mex Lober got me. Take good care of my mother. Bliss Quillen is going to . . .

The writing ended in a scrawl.

Lew looked up, wondering that he could read it at all in the faint light.

Above the cañon was the moon. It had risen above the dust and smoke of the east, and stood out white and clear in a cloudless sky.

Empty Guns

Old Sam Winthrop strode jauntily out of his general store to the little porch in front of it, where the town loafers usually sat to whittle up Sam's boxes and brag about the big things they had done or were going to do. Sam was a small, wiry, and hard-bitten rider of the range who had retired from his big ranch in order to give his young niece the advantages of education and culture. He considered Elk City, with its single street of weather-beaten buildings and its tiny schoolhouse, to be the height of educational and cultural perfection.

A tall cattleman, with a long face and iron-gray hair, came dashing up the street on a big, bay gelding. He jumped off the horse, threw two half hitches around a post, and walked awkwardly toward the store in his high-heeled boots. His leather chaps and huge, four-gallon hat were covered with gray dust, and it had gathered over his eyebrows and in the hollow places of his cheeks. He looked as though he had ridden hard and far. The ugly black handle of a Colt .45 protruded from a leather holster at his side.

Howdy, Ed," greeted old Sam as the other approached. "Goin' to a fire or a funeral?"

"Sam, I guess it's going to be a funeral,"

groaned the other. "It's either mine or that mangy coyote of a Mace Baxter's. I'll shoot daylight through that imp of hell before I'm a . . ."

"Whoa!" shouted Sam. "What's eatin' you, anyway? Why, you old leather-hided cowpoke, you can't shoot it out with Mace. He's a shade quicker than greased lightning, and can plug dollars as fast as you can toss 'em in the air. What in hell have you been messin' around with him for? He's pizen, Ed. He's a rattlesnake if there ever was one, only a rattlesnake's a gentleman beside Mace Baxter."

Ed Allison, the owner of the big Diamond F spread, pulled off his hat and mopped his sweating brow and dusty face with a red bandanna.

"It ain't me at all, Sam," he said. "I wouldn't have nothin' to do with the skunk except with a rope thrown over a cottonwood limb. It's that kid, Chuck Easton. He's a-comin' hell for leather to commit suicide at the end of Mace Baxter's shootin' iron."

"What are you talkin' about, anyway?" ejaculated Sam.

"Well, you see, Sam, mebbe you ain't kept in touch with the folks over in the Windy River country lately, but you know the trouble Mace had with Chuck's dad about five years ago. It started when Mace got too free with his branding iron, and then came to a head over that north section of hay land that grows blue-joint as high as your head. Mace didn't have a leg to stand on, and Bill beat him in the lawsuit they had over it.

"Then Bill was found dead with a bullet between the eyes. Of course, everyone suspected Mace, but we couldn't prove nothin' and he didn't even stand trial. Chuck's mother died a year later, and the boy has been living with an uncle over on Whiteclay ever since. Mace grabbed the land and said it was his. Well, Chuck came of age last spring, and he started up the old ranch with some cattle his uncle gave him. Mace sent Smoky Johnson over and told Chuck to keep off that north section, and Chuck dusted Smoky's pants for him and sent him home, howlin' like a buck Sioux at a dog feast. Chuck is a hot-headed kid, but he's as true blue a young wildcat as ever grew up on the range.

"Now that skunk of a Mace is too wise to start a fight. So he schemes out how to make Chuck bring a fight to him. Then he can kill in self-defense. At least he'll make it look like that. Chuck is sweet on that young schoolma'am that teaches over on the branch. The schoolhouse was built on Mace's land. Well, this morning Mace walks in and says school is out. He says they can take the damned building off his land and keep it off. I suppose maybe he's got a right to do it, but, goshamighty, anybody let's 'em build a schoolhouse should be damned glad to get it. Mace run all the kids out of the school, and, when the girl flares up at him, he slaps her face good."

Sam lifted up his one good eye and swore great oaths to high heaven. They were oaths both eloquent and profane, and they came from the heart.

"Then he says, casual-like," Ed continued, "that he was coming over here to Elk City, and would be in the Last Chance saloon if any of the school board cared to see him."

"Yeah," remarked Sam quietly, "he knew well enough who would come . . . the damned rattlesnake."

"Sure he did. I learned about it when young Chuck came ridin' past my place for home. He was goin' to get a gun. So I hits the trail, Sam, and I'm gunnin' for that ornery skunk if it's the last thing I ever do. Bill Easton was my friend, and I ain't going to let Mace Baxter do in his boy. I'm old, Sam, and I'm tough, and I'm going to pick a fight with that mean cuss and shoot him dead. It's just like finding a rattlesnake and stomping on its head."

"Yeah," said Sam, "I eat 'em for breakfast." Savagely he bit off a liberal chew of tobacco and his words were somewhat indistinct until the chew was settled and going smoothly. "Now, looky here, Ed, this ain't a time to rush into a fight, 'cause, if you do, the chances are we will carry you home on a shutter. This wants brains and not brawn, Ed. You got the brawn, all right, but . . ."

"Oh, yeah?" interrupted Ed with a slight grin. "Yeah? I got the brawn, and I suppose you got the brains."

"Sure. Now you're talkin'. You see, Ed, I'm a leadin' merchant of Elk City, while you're only a pore old rancher that only has thirty thousand acres of land and five or six thousand head of measly whiteface cattle. You could have called out your army of cow waddies and come chargin' into town and taken out Mace Baxter and stretched his neck for him. But instead o' that, you come ridin' in with your six-gun in order to take up the battle of a kid. You're just like old Sir Lancelot hisself. That's you all over, Ed, and this yere community ain't rich enough to get along without a man like you. So I say it's brains instead of bullets we gotta use in this man's fight. Now, you take this young Chuck Easton . . ."

"Here he comes!" cried Ed, pointing far down the road where a thin cloud of dust announced a lone rider. He seemed to be a very tiny rider at that distance, but they could see him plainly in the clear air. "I gotta be going, Sam. If you have anything to offer, get it off your chest, because hell will be poppin' in ten minutes."

"Lemme see that gun, Ed." Sam reached out quickly and pulled the .45 from its dusty holster. He broke it and looked at the cartridges that gleamed, bright and shining and ready for business. "Are these all the cartridges you got?" he asked.

"Sure. Ain't they enough? I don't need a whole belt full to shoot one rattlesnake, Sam."

Sam snapped the cartridges into his hand, and then, with a quick motion, threw them far over the adjoining store.

"Hey!" shouted Ed. "What are you doin' there? Why, you . . . you . . ."

"Now don't get riled, Ed," Sam remarked serenely. "I told you brains is going to win out against bullets in this man's battle. Come on, now. We're going to find Mace Baxter, and you keep your mouth shut and watch your uncle Samuel. I'll show you how to pull the pizen from a rattlesnake. I eat 'em for breakfast."

Ed took his useless weapon, looked at it dolefully a moment, and then restored it to its holster. There might be time enough to get more cartridges at the hardware store, but—he glanced down the road, and then followed Sam into the Last Chance.

Three cow waddies from the C Cross were playing roulette with a professional gambler from Wimbleton. They seemed to be experiencing considerable profane hilarity as their monthly wages went the way of all flesh. Two cattlemen were standing at the far end of the bar, discussing something in a low tone. Adolph Schultz, the bartender, in a dirty apron was arranging glasses and decanters against the showy mirror that was the pride of Elk City and the Last Chance.

Standing with his back to the bar, his thin lips pressed into a straight line, his keen, black eyes peering steadily into the street, stood Mace Baxter. He was a dark, thin, nervous man whose slightest motion showed the speed that had made him famous as a gunman and a killer.

His lean jaws were working steadily, and occasionally he turned and spat into a box of sawdust by the bar. A heavy Colt swung at his right side; it was a vicious, notorious six-gun that some said carried five notches in the handle, and some said six. No one had ever seen it closely enough to make sure, and Mace did not enlighten them.

He glanced quickly at Ed and Sam as they entered, but did not return Sam's cheerful: "Howdy." Mace Baxter was waiting silently and expectantly, and there was death in his murderous heart.

"A couple of rye highs," ordered Sam as he and Ed stepped to the bar. "As I was sayin' before we came in, Ed, most of these old gun-toters wasn't all they was cracked up to be. You know how a story goes. It swells up just like a black calf born in the dark o' the moon. Now I never did know a gunman that was worth a cuss. He was always a sneak and a measly coward."

Mace Baxter shot a black glance at Sam, who drank part of his highball serenely and then smacked his lips. Ed stared wonderingly at his friend. Sam had no gun. Ed's weapon was empty, and yet Sam seemed bent on picking a quarrel with the fastest killer in the whole country.

"Now you take the draw," Sam went on. "I wasn't never so hot on the draw, but I beat Dutch Brannigan who had a reputation a yard long and a mile wide. These fellers is all right at a rodeo, but when it comes to gettin' a gun out of leather quicker'n the other fellow, they just natcherly get scared and fold up and take it in the gizzard."

"Like Dutch Brannigan?" ventured Ed, who had happened to be present when that bully came to an untimely and unlamented end of the trail.

"Yeah, just like Dutch Brannigan."

Sam finished his highball and again smacked his lips with a sound like the crack of a miniature pistol. "Now you take all this fancy stuff like shootin' in a mirror and the roll, and all that hooey," he went on. "There ain't nothin' to it. It's nice enough at a rodeo where you can show off with a passel o' pretty gals lookin' on, but it ain't of no practical value."

He leaned leisurely against the bar and eyed the decanters wistfully. Ed glanced uneasily at the street where, at any moment, the enraged Chuck Easton would come riding into view.

"There's all this talk about the roll," continued Sam. "It makes me laugh. Who o' these big killers knows how to work the roll? Gimme that gun, Ed, and I'll show you how it's done." He jerked the weapon from Ed's holster and held it out over the bar. "Now, looky here! Here am I holding this gun by the barrel. It looks innocent enough, yet my finger is under the trigger guard, and all of a sudden . . ."

The gun spun so quickly the eye could scarcely follow it. Sam's thumb caught the hammer that fell with a loud *click*. The whole operation had taken quite less than a second.

"Whoa, there!" shouted Adolph. "What are ya tryin' to do? Bust that mirror? Dang it all, you fellows had better look out. How'd you know that gun ain't loaded?"

"Shucks." Sam grinned. "None of these old birds ever carried a loaded gun. It's all a bluff."

He spun the weapon again and again, thumbing the hammer with a speed and precision that were uncanny. Mex was watching him with interest, for this was handling a gun in a way that he could appreciate.

Ed could not fathom Sam's game. He thought his friend had intended having the weapon ready to shove into the ribs of the gunman as soon as Chuck appeared, and then show it was unloaded as a joke. Ed had seen him do things just as crazy. But now Sam had shown that he was unarmed and harmless.

"Knowing how to do the roll and then doing it, when a feller is all excited about shootin' for business, is a whole lot different," went on Sam.

"That ornery Blake Waldron tried it on the sheriff over at Big Springs. He pretended to hand out the gun, butt first, when the sheriff had the drop on him, and then tried to work the roll. What happened? He got all mussed up with a Forty-Four slug through a lung. Somehow, these yere gunmen always seem to get theirs, and they get it from some young feller that don't know nothin' about fancy tricks with a gun. It always happens. I ain't never seen it fail."

It dawned on Ed that Sam was trying to wreck the nerve of the killer who stood near him. Ed grinned then. He was about to add an experience of his own when a sweating, blowing horse galloped into view and drew up sharply before the hitch rack across the street.

Mace Baxter stirred and hooked his right thumb in his belt just above the black handle of his .45.

A young man dismounted easily from the horse and threw the reins over the hitch rack. Tall, well-formed, with shoulder muscles rippling beneath a close-fitting shirt, he was a fine specimen of Western manhood as he stood pounding the gray dust from his clothes and big hat.

He pulled off the saddle, unfastened a blanket that was rolled behind it, and then threw the blanket over the exhausted animal. He drew his gun, looked at it carefully, whirled the cylinder, and then thrust it back into the holster. Drawing his hat low over his fine brow, he turned and walked steadily toward the Last Chance.

The cowboys had stopped playing roulette and were watching Mace, as though they sensed the approaching tragedy.

The low conversation at the end of the bar ceased.

"Now you take Wes Hagen," Sam was saying. "He always worked like this. Damn this gun anyway, Ed. It ain't worth shucks. I can't do nothin' with it. Let's see. . . ." He reached out suddenly, seized the handle of Mace's Colt, and snatched the weapon from the holster. "Lemme take your gun a minute, Mace," he said serenely. "Now this is something like. You see, when you want to do the roll, you gotta . . ."

Like a bomb exploding, Mace came out of his tense, motionless position that reminded Ed of a cat watching for a mouse.

"Damn you!" he cried. "Gimme that gun!" One brown paw shot out, clutched the diminutive Sam by the shoulder, and turned him around. "Gimme that gun!"

Chuck Easton flung wide the door and strode into the room. His head was up and his eyes were on the man he had come to kill.

Mace was scuffling with Sam, who twisted and turned and held onto the weapon. "Gimme that gun!" Mace screamed as he swung Sam from side to side, too excited and angry to act intelligently.

Ed was on the point of lending a hand to his friend, but he knew Sam was perfectly capable of taking care of himself in a rough-and-tumble row. Taking the killer's gun away from him wouldn't end this fight, anyway. The feud between Mace Baxter and Chuck Easton had reached the point where it must be fought out with blazing guns and hot lead, and no temporary respite would be of any help to Chuck.

"What the hell, Mace?" Sam expostulated. "What's the matter with you, anyway? I was just goin' to show Ed something with your weapon. I wasn't going to eat the damned thing. There! Take it, if your all so het up about it. You're a hell of a neighbor and friend."

He shoved the gun into its holster and Mace turned quickly to confront Chuck Easton. He made a slight movement with his hand as though to make sure that his .45 was there, but he evidently thought better of it. He stood, resting his thumb lightly on his heavy belt. His fingers were slightly curved—an apparently innocent position to which no one could object—thumb hooked over belt, fingers slightly curved above the black handle of the gun. It was a position from which that gun could leap from the holster and send forth flaming death within a split second. The weight of the weapon in its proper place seemed to restore all his cool, stoical confidence. He stood, looking into the angry blue eyes of the young man before him without a sign that this was anything more than a casual meeting.

Ed stood, staring with wide eyes. He wanted to do something—anything—but no plan of action presented itself to him. Sam had disarmed him. Sam also had tried to disarm Mace—and had failed. Ed continued to stare at the two actors in this drama of death that was being played out before him, his hand mechanically fumbling for the gun that should have been hanging at his side.

Sam was standing near Chuck, watching intently with his one bright eye. Ed wondered if the little man still thought he could prevent the slaughter.

Chuck Easton's jaw was hard set and he spoke between clenched teeth. He was trembling with suppressed rage as he faced this killer who he had hated since childhood. Evidently he had prepared a little speech.

"Mace Baxter," he gritted, "you're sitting on the lid of hell right now, and it's going to swing in and let you through. When you went to that schoolhouse this morning, you signed your death warrant. You dirty, low-lived, sneaking, cowardly hound! Draw your gun!"

His hand shot out, and he slapped the dark face before him with open palm. It was a blow that meant flaming guns in the West, and Ed watched for the lightning draw that would end Chuck's earthly career. But Mace did not draw.

It was plain that the killer's plan had been

carefully made. Evidently he intended to provoke Chuck into drawing first, and then he could kill in self-defense. Otherwise, it might go hard with him in a country where his talents with a six-gun were well known.

Calmly, without speaking, with his right hand still in that dangerous position at his side, he leaned forward and sent a stream of tobacco juice over Chuck's boots.

"That for you," he said.

Chuck's face flamed crimson. He was seeing red. Trembling with rage, he slapped the leering face before him again and again.

"You . . . you hound!" he cried "I could overlook all you did to my father and me, but I'll get you for what you did to Ellen Wilson if I have to swing for it. Draw, you . . . you damned coward!"

Mace jerked his head to one side as Chuck struck again. Then he leaned forward and spat fairly in the boy's face.

With a howl, Chuck reached for his weapon. Gone was his intention to make Mace draw first. He fumbled for a moment, and then his gun came from the holster.

Like a striking snake, the curved hand of the killer flashed downward. The big Colt leaped out as if by magic. There was a dull *click* and then another, as the hammer was fanned by a lightning thumb.

Chuck's gun roared!

Mace spun half around and clutched the bar with his left hand. His Colt fell from nerveless fingers and his right arm dropped, limp and useless, at his side.

Sam had leaped at the first shot. He grabbed Chuck's gun hand and forced it straight down, and the second bullet was fired into the floor.

"Hold on, kid!" Sam cried. "Don't shoot any more. You've busted his arm. It's all right! You got him fair an' square."

Mace was staring at the young man with wide eyes and open mouth, and Ed muttered: "The best laid plans o' mice and men gang aft all blooey."

Mace looked at his weapon, which was lying on the floor. A thin stream of blood trickled down over his hand and fingers and began dripping into the box of sawdust by the bar.

The room was in an uproar with everybody shouting at once. The men in the saloon gathered about Mace and Chuck, and others came running in.

Adolph was howling at Chuck.

"You damn' fool!" he fumed. "You almost busted my mirror. Get out of here, if you want to go gunning. This is a orderly, peaceful saloon and not a damned battlefield. I imported that mirror all the way from Berlin, France, and I ain't going to have it shot full of holes, not by a danged sight."

Sam cut away the killer's sleeve and examined the wound.

"Mace, your elbow's clean shattered and busted," he cried sorrowfully. "You ain't going to do no more quick draw stuff. Your big day is over, an' your arm will be stiff as a poker all the rest o' your life. Now git to the doc as fast as you can heel it, and let him fix you up with some splints. Your little game didn't work, Mace. It's like my old grandmother used to say about a whistlin' gal and a crowin' hen. They always come to some bad end."

Mace's dark face was a greenish tinge. Evidently he was in great pain, but he set his lips tightly and said nothing as he walked firmly to the door and into the street.

"Son, you won't have no more trouble with that skunk," Ed was saying. "All you have to look out for is ambush, and I don't think he'll try that. 'Cause, if you should turn up missing, we will hang him first and find out about it afterwards. He knows it, too. No one will be afraid of him now. The rattlesnake sure lost his fangs today."

Chuck slowly shoved his gun into the holster and mopped his brow.

"I . . . I suppose I ought to be arrested," he choked. "I . . . I didn't mean to draw first, but I lost my temper. . . ."

"What are you talking about, son?" Ed assured him. "Drawin' a gun ain't everything. Mace had his six-shooter out and clicked it twice before yours cleared leather. It's a clear case of self-defense. Who would expect you to stand still, with Mace clickin' at you? How could you know his gun wasn't loaded? Anyway, he ain't dead, dang it."

A C Cross cowboy was talking in a loud voice. "Whoever would have thought Mace would git in a fight with an empty gun?" he wondered. "I never thought anyone would be that keerless."

"Shucks, that ain't nothin'," explained Sam. "It's just like I told Adolph. None o' these old killers ever carried a loaded gun. It was all bluff. I've knowed it for years."

A few minutes later Ed and Sam went swinging cheerfully down the street, toward the store.

"You was sure right, Sam," Ed declared with a wide grin. "It was brains against bullets, and the brains was all on our side. You sneaked the cartridges out o' that gun of his slicker than grease. I didn't see you do it, and I didn't even know what the hell you was tryin' to do. Gimme back that gun now, and I promise not to get into mischief with it."

He took the weapon Sam handed him, and then stopped still and stared.

"What the hell!" he exclaimed. "This ain't my gun. It's got five . . . six . . . seven notches in the handle. Why, it belongs to Mace, and that seventh notch must have been for Bill Easton. I see,

Sam, I see! You danged old rooster, you switched guns on Mace when you was in that scuffle. I'll have to hand it to you, boy. You sure know how to draw the pizen from rattlesnakes."

"Yeah," said Sam modestly. "I eat 'em for breakfast."

A Girl Is Like a Colt

At first, after the blow had fallen, Jim Hunt tried to go about the business of his ranch as if nothing had happened. He sent his cowboys upcountry and downcountry, bearing down on the work, but the letter he had just received from the girl in Denver milled incessantly through his mind.

It was just a brief, not very eloquent letter, such as a girl writes who wishes to let a man down as gently as may be. The girl—her name was Alice—expressed her lasting admiration for Jim and hoped he would agree that they had perhaps been headlong and somewhat silly. But Hunt already knew that an outstanding rival named Chalmers had now been in Denver more than a month. Hunt had done pretty well in cattle, but he could not compete with the monumental wealth of Chalmers, and now he read the cards without any difficulty.

So, presently, he went into his ranch house to the unhappy job of writing a terminal message to the girl.

It was slow going, but the wire was nearly composed by the time he was interrupted by his lanky range foreman, Ed Parr. Parr leaned over Jim's shoulder to give his unconcealed interest to Jim's literary effort.

"What the heck," Hunt demanded, "you think you're doing?"

Ed Parr frowned judicially, and read Jim's telegram aloud: " 'If that is what you want, I wish you all happiness stop If ever you want me or need me, you have only to say so stop Devoted love . . .' What's the idea you keep saying 'stop'? It sounds like you was trying to talk and somebody was tickling you."

Hunt snorted. But he let down, feeling the need of consolation and advice. "Outside of that, don't you think . . . ?"

"Outside of that I think you got daisies in your hair. Where you make your mistake, you lay down and let that girl ride over you. You . . ."

"Do you know what I figure?" Hunt demanded. "Nothing ever made me so sick in my life. Chalmers's money is responsible for this. I feel just like he had outbid me and bought her."

"Looks more like it was your own fault. Take breaking a colt. How did you teach that roan bronc' to come running up to you when he sees the halter? Why, you popped a forty-foot black-snake around him until he thought he was entirely surrounded by serious explosions, and . . ."

"For God's sake, will you shut up?"

Parr shrugged. "All right. But you're a sucker to send a wire like that. Bang goes sixty-five cents, just to forward a kind of mooing sound."

"Darned if I know what to send."

"Send for a drink. No, here, I'll get it myself. Next thing, you stick a quart bottle in your boot and go to town. You got to get in and wire Schuyler, if you aim to outbid Murphy for them six thousand acres on the Taboose."

"To hell with it."

"With Murphy bidding only four and a half an acre, you can anyway up him two bits. Go on to town. And if you turn up here sober inside of four days, I aim to send you fishing."

For once the fire-eating Jim Hunt obeyed his employee. He went to town with a bottle in his boot, and it was two days before he turned up at his ranch again, feeling worse than ever.

"You know how I feel?" he asked Parr from the depths of gloom. "I feel like that rich fellow just outbid me, and as good as bought her."

Ed Parr said: "Well, I varnished your fish pole."

Hunt went fishing, and this time was gone a week. But he returned, looking lower than ever.

"You know what I figure?" he told Parr. "It's just the same as if Chalmers went to work and he . . ."

"Yeah, he just outbid you and bought her. You already told me that. Well, there's some mail for you, and a couple telegrams. I opened one telegram, thinking it was about that Taboose land. It wasn't. But, say! She's plenty sore, to judge by her wire."

"*Her* wire? Let's see it!"

Parr rummaged, and produced the yellow sheet. Six surprising words stared up at Jim Hunt:

Hunt looked blank. "Funny. I didn't send her any word."

Parr considered. "Maybe she explains in this other telegram. I didn't dast open it, after the first one blew up in my face."

Hunt ripped open the second wire, and stared at it:

NO I DON'T FORGIVE MY LETTER
FOLLOWS ALICE

"Here's a letter, seems like from her," Parr prompted. Hunt tore open the envelope.

"She wants me to forgive her," he said as if speaking of a miracle. "Chalmers is out, and I'm ace high again." Abruptly bafflement crossed his face. "Dog-goned if I get it. She talks like I sent her a message of some kind . . . and I did no such a thing. Parr"—he suddenly turned fiercely on his foreman—"I bet you wired that girl!"

"Who, me? And pay for it myself?"

"I'll soon find out if you did! I'm going in to talk to the telegraph people. Of all the infernal nerve . . ."

Jim Hunt had Parr belligerently defensive by the time they reached the town. They strode, steaming, into the telegraph office.

"Where's that wire Parr sent out of here last week?"

"We haven't any, Mister Hunt. Parr hasn't been in here."

Hunt faltered, nonplussed, and Parr played his card. "Well, then, where's the wire Hunt sent?"

"I tell you," Hunt raved, "I know if I sent a wire or not!"

"You mean to say you was so illuminated you didn't even wire Schuyler about the Taboose land?"

"Sure I wired Schuyler, but . . ."

Parr jerked a carbon copy from the clerk's hands, and as he read the dried leather of his face slowly crinkled. "I mind you said you figured that rich feller was bidding you out of the girl. You're a game one, though, to try to beat him with such a slim boost as this."

Hunt snatched the copy of the wire from Parr. He stared at it for a long minute as if he could not believe his eyes, then his hands went slack and the paper fluttered to the floor.

From the floor looked up the words that had reached across two states to astound a girl, infuriate her, half break her heart, and finally bring her back to the man she had decided to forget:

MISS ALICE HANCOCK
DENVER COLO
    I RAISE HIS BID FIFTEEN CENTS

Dead Man's Ambush

Two slightly intoxicated cowboys were singing as they rode homeward along a dusty trail. Behind them rattled a buckboard covered with a canvas top, home-made, a small edition of the covered wagon of historic fame. An old man sat hunched in the driver's seat, the reins flapping as the team trotted steadily. Over the man's eyes were black glasses that hid not only the eyes themselves, but also an ugly scar extending across the bridge of his nose.

He sniffed as the dust drifted back to him. Then he caught a snatch of the song—and frowned. That song had been dinned into his ears for two decades, and he heard it again with deep resentment:

> Now Jason Burke was a hero's name,
> And a lawman bold was he;
> Sometimes he used lead, but always his
>   head,
> In his battle with outlawry.

Unconsciously the driver of the buckboard straightened. The song was about him, or at least it was about the Jason Burke who once rode the range in a relentless warfare against lawlessness—about the Jason Burke who had eyes. The song was composed by Squawky Jones, a troubadour of cattle towns and saloons in the olden days. Squawky went from place to place, singing his original doggerels about the hard-riding, hard-shooting men of the range land. Unaware that the hero of the ditty rode close behind, the cowboys sang another of the thirty-odd verses:

> He tricked Billy Simms, he shot Faro
>   Joe,
> He put a slug through Hangman Ball;
> Of a host of bold rangers that rode on
>   the trail,
> Jason Burke was the boldest of all.

The team slowed to a walk, and then stopped. Well trained, that was their way of telling their blind master they had come to a fork in the trail. Knowing the range as he knew the rooms in his little home, Burke could find his way over the rolling prairie without hesitation. He always knew exactly where he was.

Today he took the road to the left, gratefully leaving the cowboys and their song, and presently the team stopped at a wire gate. Springing lightly to the ground, the old ex-sheriff opened the gate with sure hand. The team went through obediently, and a moment later he was back on the seat with the reins flapping loosely.

He was on Reverse J6 land now, and Mrs. Marvin was one of his sure customers. She always bought something out of his wagon, and sometimes he suspected they were things she really didn't need. But people were like that in this great range land that he loved with deep devotion. They were not only customers; they were neighbors and friends.

As he drove up before the door, someone ran out and greeted him.

"Howdy, Sheriff!"

Everyone still called him that, although now it was but a hollow title of courtesy. The title, Sheriff, meant something in the old days.

"Howdy, Ellen." He recognized every voice as another would recognize a face. "My, my, but you must have quite growed up. 'Most eighteen, ain't you? I'd shore like to see that pretty face. Where's your ma?"

"In town. Dad and all the boys are at the roundup. But I know what Mother wants. One of those big kettles, a pair of scissors like she got last time, a coffee pot, and an alarm clock."

"All right, Ellen. I'll get 'em. Only two clocks left. They're shore gettin' scarce since the war."

He stepped over the seat into the wagon, where he could put his hand instantly on any of the hundred-odd items he peddled from ranch to ranch.

The county board had offered Burke a pension

after Charley Great Horse, the Cheyenne outlaw, had fired the shot that forever ended his career as a lawman. But Jason Burke refused money that smacked of charity. The fact that he lost his eyes in the service of the county mattered not at all. He was paid to take chances, he said. When the game went against him, he wasn't helping himself to any free chips.

"A big kettle," he repeated aloud. "Does your ma want the one for three dollars, or the heavy one for four twenty-five?"

"The one for four twenty-five, I'm sure. And, Sheriff Burke, do you have any brooms?"

"Have I got brooms?" He chuckled. "I just got in a whole bundle of 'em. Twenty-eight dollars' worth is what I got left. If you buy one, I'll have twenty-seven dollars' worth to sweep out the rest of the county."

He chuckled again as he emerged from the interior of the wagon.

"Here you are, young lady. Kettle, scissors, coffee pot, clock, and broom. Your dad can pay me sometime when he's in town, and many thanks. Tell him the bill is nine twenty-five in case I forget."

His keen ear caught the sound of a soft step coming up behind the girl. He turned his head.

"Sheriff Burke," came a guttural voice. "Fine day."

"Yes. It's you, is it, Charley?"

He had recognized the voice of Charley Great Horse, the outlaw who was responsible for his blindness.

"Yes, me, Charley. No hard feelings, Sheriff?"

"No, there are no hard feelings, Charley. You know I was always your friend. How are you gettin' along?"

Many times had the two met since the shooting. Charley was still an outlaw, hiding somewhere in the mountains, but Jason Burke was no longer a lawman. He had great sympathy for this untutored Indian whose greatest crime was to kill a white trapper who had robbed him of his squaw.

"Me get along fine. Got swell shack in hills. Pan out gold in stream. No one knows but me. Friends buy most what I need. I want kettle like girl has."

"All right, Charley."

The transaction was made, the Indian paying in coin.

"Big dam on river will be blown up tonight," Charley remarked as though making casual conversation.

Jason Burke started.

"What did you say, Charley? Do you mean Preston Dam? Who's gonna blow it up?"

After a moment of silence Charley spoke again. "Japs ran away from prison camps four suns ago."

"I know it. Twenty-two of 'em. They're bad

hombres, Charley. All are army men from Japan, imported a few years ago for sabotage in case of war. Where are they?"

"In Shaween Mountains."

"The Shaweens, eh? Good hidin' place. I'll report it. But what about the dam?"

"Japs going to rob Cincona Mine today. Maybe already. Steal load of dynamite and truck. Drive to dam by midnight. Blow it to sky."

"Sheriff Burke!" cried Ellen. "If they do that, they'll flood the whole valley and the towns. Hundreds of people will be drowned!"

"Yes, and the oil wells and big refinery will be wiped out. That would be a real blow they can strike for the son o' heaven. It's got to be stopped, but how are we goin' to do it?"

Again came the low voice of the Indian. "Charley go now. No can help."

"That's right, Charley, but many thanks. But stay away from them Japs. They'll prob'ly shoot you in the back if they get a chance."

"Me heard them talking in American, but they no saw Charley. I tell you about it, Sheriff Burke. I am American."

"I understand, Charley, and you're a real American. This will be a big thing if we can stop 'em, and I'll make the governor sign a pardon for you if I have to shove a gun under his nose. So long, Charley, and the best of luck."

Again there were the soft padding footsteps,

and Burke knew the Indian was on his way back to the mountains.

"Ellen," he said, and his voice had the tense ring of the old Sheriff Jason Burke, "get on a horse an' ride like . . . like sixty . . . to the Circle Seven. The telephone line runs past there. Call Sheriff Hal Stanton an' tell him what's up."

"But will there be time?"

He remained silent a moment, thinking. "No, there won't, Ellen. They never can get from town to Preston Dam before midnight. We gotta stop those Japs before they get out of the hills. Tell Hal to forget that danged automobile of his, an' drum up a posse on horses. They can come through the rough country over the wash to that deep cut where the road comes out of the hills. If they beat the Japs to it, they can round 'em up. If they're too late, there'll be Hades poppin' when that dam goes out."

Without a word Ellen ran to the corral, and seconds later she was in the saddle ready to go.

"I gotta get men," Jason Burke told her. "One way or another we must hold them Japs in the cut till Hal an' his posse gets there. The road's only a few feet wide, an' three or four men can hold up an army with rifles. We gotta do it."

"But Sheriff Burke," she cried, "what can you do? You . . ." She hesitated.

"Go on an' say it, gal," he said bitterly. "What can a man do when he's old and blind? I don't know, but I'll have time to go around by the Lazy S, an' still reach the cut before dark. Mebbe some of the boys didn't go to the roundup. The Japs will have to come down early if they reach the dam by midnight. Some of 'em must be pretty smart . . . hid up in the Shaween Mountains while the Army men are scourin' the hills sixty miles away. Ride like heck, Ellen. Tell Hal to get there before dark or we're sunk."

He turned into the trail leading toward the hills, and his voice cracked like a whiplash as he urged the team to its utmost speed. He knew by the feel of the air that the sun already was low in the west. The buckboard bounded over the rough trail with a banging of pots and pans, and Burke clung to the seat as he cheered on the team. He would have to go fast if he took time to stop at the Lazy S for men.

In spite of his aversion to the old song, some of its verses were running through his head as the team thundered along the trail:

> Whoever steals cattle, whoever robs
>   banks,
> Whoever takes up outlaw ways,
> Will face Jason Burke in the wink of an
>   eye,
> And learn that crime never pays.

The team stopped so suddenly Burke was nearly thrown from the seat. Another wire gate.

He opened it, and turned to the right. Again he urged the horses to a run.

> For Jason Burke is a man of the law,
> His hand is as swift and as sure
> As the swoop of an eagle making a kill,
> For crime he will give a lead cure.

The absurdity of the situation struck him forcibly, and his face saddened. He was old and blind, yet one of the big moments of his life had come to him. It was not merely a case of rustlers taking someone's cattle, or a saloon fight, or an ordinary hold-up. It was a real part in a great war. A valley of irrigated farms producing food and meat was at stake and a great oil field and refinery that sent solid trainloads of tank cars to the West Coast. Oil for ships, gasoline for tanks and trucks and airplanes from Alaska to Australia. A score of trained Japanese with guns and dynamite were after that oil field, and there was only a blind old man to stop them.

Burke's voice took on a note of harshness as he shouted to the team, although they were already doing their utmost. Suppose no one was at home on the Lazy S? What would he do?

> His wits are as sharp as a keen Bowie
>   knife,
> His gun is as deadly as sin;

When an outlaw gets tough on the
   rolling prairie,
 Old Jason will gather him in.

Again the team came to a sudden stop. It was a trail this time that turned to the Lazy S. The air was growing cooler, and Burke knew the sun was settling down behind the hills. Yet he felt there was still time.

Whatever the cost, those Japanese must be held at the cut where the road came down from the mountains. It was a perfect spot, high, sloping banks on each side covered with bushes. Fifty or more men could take cover there, and command the road as perfectly as with a battery of artillery.

Jason Burke talked to the team as it galloped toward the Lazy S. All he needed was a few men with rifles, and he could do the trick. He had a plan for stopping that truck with its dynamite and its Japanese. . . .

All had gone well for the escaped Japanese prisoners. The captured truck lumbered down over the rocky road that descended sharply as it left the mountains. In it were twenty-two men. Small men, with grim, yellow-brown faces. Two of them carried rifles that they had captured from the Cincona Mine. They had tied up the five miners, and filled the truck nearly half full of dynamite. It was enough to blow up a dozen Preston Dams.

Sueo Nogura was in command. He was an army officer with decorations and a record in Japan. A graduate of an American university, he had been sent back to the United States to lead a swift campaign of destroying shipyards, factories, and oil refineries, and to set fires throughout the forest region. The blowing up of the important Preston Dam was part of the original plan that had been delayed when Nogura and his fellows were arrested at the beginning of the war. His hatred for Americans was intense, but especially bitter was his feeling for the men of Japanese ancestry who had proved to be eyes and ears for the F.B.I. Nogura could not understand how love for freedom and country could be greater than love of race, and the Emperor who had descended from heaven.

Sueo Nogura knew there would be no trouble planting the dynamite at the dam. Only two men were stationed there, watchmen rather than guards. Who would suspect sabotage in such an out-of-the-way place? The stupid Americans of the West had no sense. It was easy for the Japanese to trick them.

The truck rounded a curve in a long cut bordered by high, sloping banks covered with sumac and sun berry and buffalo bushes.

Suddenly the driver sounded a warning on the siren and stopped the truck with a jerk. Squarely across the road, blocking it completely, was a team of horses and a canvas-covered wagon. In the seat was an old man, head bowed, a pair of black glasses over his eyes.

Nogura knew him for a blind peddler who traveled from ranch to ranch, selling pots and pans. Doubtless the man was lost.

"Turn your team, blind man!" he called. "You are across the road! Turn to the left and go straight ahead!"

The man did not move. Nogura jumped off the truck and ran over to the wagon.

"Start your team, I say. Turn to the left, and you will be in the middle of the road. Be quick! We are in a hurry."

For answer the old man held up his hand. Then he called out in a ringing voice: "Don't shoot till I tell you, men."

Nogura glanced up at the sides of the cut. Then his small eyes spread wide and his jaw dropped. From the bushes on both sides of the truck he saw black, small, ugly cylinders that struck terror to his heart.

One of the men in the back of the truck cried out.

"We run into ambush! Rifles are all around us. Captain, we are surrounded!"

As though frozen to his place, Nogura did not move. He was willing to die for the Emperor, but what could he do with that ring of firearms around him? The truck couldn't be turned in that narrow road and they couldn't ride over the wagon of the blind man in a quick getaway.

Being returned to a concentration camp, where he and his men would be well housed and well fed, was better than meeting a certain and flaming death from that score of guns. Yes, Sueo Nogura was willing to die for the Emperor, and his men, also, but the officer decided it was the better part of wisdom to postpone the event till a later day.

"Put your hands up high," commanded the blind man.

Nogura and his men obeyed, and remained without moving.

"Stay where you are!" the peddler ordered. "If you make one move, you'll be filled so full of lead you'll never see the risin' sun again." Then he lifted his voice. "Hold 'em where they are, men. We'll have our orders as quick as the sheriff gets here. Till he comes, we're just stayin' where we are. Shoot any man that puts down his hands. We ain't takin' any chances."

The slow minutes dragged by. They seemed hours to the prisoners who had failed in their mission when success seemed so certain. Nogura wondered if he could stealthily light a fuse and explode the dynamite. But what good would it do? He and his men would be blown to atoms and the only damage would be a hole in the road. If he had only been near enough to the dam!

From far away came a crashing in the brush, and then the sound of horses' hoofs on the road.

A group of grim men rode up. One of them wore a sheriff's badge.

"Here they are!" he shouted. "Jason's got 'em surrounded and hog-tied. Come on, you Japs. You're goin' back where Uncle Sam wants you. Pretty smart, ain't you? But not quite smart enough. I'm sorry we can't hang you, but the Army won't stand for it."

Ten minutes later the prisoners were sitting in the bottom of the truck securely handcuffed. Without a word of protest they were driven away by eight guards.

The other members of the posse gathered about Jason. One of them led his team around into the middle of the road, but they knew this was courtesy rather than necessity. The old man knew exactly where he was and what to do.

"We'll ride back with you, Jason," the sheriff said. "You sure done yourself proud, old-timer. Somebody ought to put a couple more verses to that old song about you. I'd do it myself if I could think of enough words. Call in your men, and we'll go."

"Men?" queried Jason, smiling slightly. "What men?"

"Why, your gunnies in the brush yonder." He lifted his voice. "Come on in, boys. The fuss is over, and you sure did a good job."

There was no response, and no movement in the bushes.

"You gotta go an' carry 'em in, Hal," Jason said with a wide grin. "In plain English they're all dead men."

"Dead men?"

"Yeah, I suppose you can call it that. In fact, they ain't men at all, but they must look like it in the near dark. In broad daylight they're just twenty-seven dollars' worth of black-handled brooms, and you gotta carry 'em in or they won't come."

About the Author

Alan LeMay was born in Indianapolis, Indiana, and attended Stetson University in DeLand, Florida, in 1916. Following his military service, he completed his education at the University of Chicago. His short story, "Hullabaloo," appeared the month of his graduation in *Adventure* (6/30/22). He was a prolific contributor to the magazine markets in the mid-1920s. With the story, "Loan of a Gun", LeMay broke into the pages of *Collier's* (2/23/29). During the next decade he wanted nothing more than to be a gentleman rancher, and his income from writing helped support his enthusiasms which included tearing out the peach-tree orchard so he could build a polo field on his ranch outside Santee, California. It was also during this period that he wrote some of his most memorable Western novels, *Gunsight Trail* (1931), *Winter Range* (1932), *Cattle Kingdom* (1933), and *Thunder in the Dust* (1934) among them. In the late 1930s he was plunged into debt because of a divorce and turned next to screenwriting, early attaching himself to Cecil B. DeMille's unit at Paramount Pictures. LeMay continued to write original screenplays through the 1940s, and on one occasion even directed the film based on his screenplay.

The Searchers (1954) is regarded by many as LeMay's masterpiece. It possesses a graphic sense of place; it etches deeply the feats of human endurance that LeMay tended to admire in the American spirit; and it has that characteristic suggestiveness of tremendous depths and untold stories developed in his long apprenticeship writing short stories. A subtext often rides on a snatch of dialogue or flashes in a laconic observation. It was followed by such classic Western novels as *The Unforgiven* (1957) and *By Dim and Flaring Lamps* (1962).

Additional Copyright Information

Center Point Large Print
600 Brooks Road / PO Box 1
Thorndike, ME 04986-0001 USA

(207) 568-3717

US & Canada:
1 800 929-9108
www.centerpointlargeprint.com